THE BURTONS

were a close-knit family.
They had to be to survive.
The Indians hated them because Sam
Burton's wife had left her tribe to
live among the white men.
The townspeople hated them because
the Burtons were a family of half-breeds.
But the Burtons were secure among
themselves—until the hate began to
spread like an uncontrolled brushfire.
The inferno of hate threatened to
consume the Burton family and set
brother against brother.

Also By Clair Huffaker

NOBODY LOVES A DRUNKEN INDIAN

FLAMING LANCE

By Clair Huffaker

PAPERBACK LIBRARY
New York

PAPERBACK LIBRARY EDITION

First Printing: March, 1970

To my son, whose name is Lance—with a love constantly flaming.

This Paperback Library Edition is published by arrangement
with Simon & Schuster, Inc.

Paperback Library is a division of Coronet Communications, Inc.
Its trademark, consisting of the words "Paperback Library" ac-
companied by an open book, is registered in the United States
Patent Office. *Coronet Communications, Inc., 315 Park Avenue
South, New York, N.Y. 10010.*

CHAPTER ONE

For as long as he could remember, Clint had never before seen a rider there—a rider framed against the darkening sky on the crest of the hill that rose sharply from the grass-covered plain a mile behind the small ranch he called home.

It was that lonely on these vast, sweeping flats of west Texas.

And now, for the first time, he had seen a horseman there, silhouetted briefly at an angle to the setting sun. For perhaps three seconds the distant, somehow menacing figure had remained rock-still before he had abruptly reined his horse away and back down the hill out of sight.

Clint had no way of knowing yet, but he would forever remember this moment—this first contact with a deadly, hostile force that was still nameless and faceless.

"You see him, Pacer?" Without moving his head, he spoke softly to his brother, who was working on the corral fence a few steps behind him.

"Yeah." Then, with flat suspicion: "Didn't like the feel of him."

The two men had been refirming the corral posts, using long iron bars to knock the earth down hard around the posts where winter thaw and spring mud had loosened them. The rhythmic thump of Pacer's bar against the ground had stopped just as Clint saw the faraway man, and Clint had been pretty sure, even before Pacer's answer, that the rider had not escaped his brother's quick eye.

"Indian?"

"Yeah," Pacer grunted. "I'd say Kiowa."

"Wonder how come he didn't ride over, then." Even though Pacer's eyes remained on the area surrounding and capping the hill, Clint knew his brother had shaken his head briefly, answerless. Then the sound of Pacer's bar pounding the ground came to him once more, and Clint turned to walk to the house.

Both men knew exactly what had to be done, and they didn't have to waste time talking about it. The work had to go on. And Pa should be told.

Clint stepped onto the low, wooden porch and with one more step was inside the small, two-room house. Ma was at the fireplace, pushing the fire a little to build it up for the evening cooking. Pa was mending a bridle, sitting at the table with his bad leg stuck out straight before him, a heavy, leather-working needle moving quickly and expertly in his strong hands. They both glanced at Clint as he entered and crossed to the bucket near the cooking board that would someday, with luck, be a sink.

"Glass of water," he said.

After drinking, and realizing as he did so that it was a foolish subterfuge to keep Ma from fretting, he said, "Pa," and walked back out of the house. He could see that Pacer was keeping a sharp eye out. A tiny kangaroo rat couldn't move within half a mile without Pacer spotting it.

A few yards from the house, he waited while Pa, limping on his game leg, came toward him. Old Stonewall Burton, he was called by most. It was a nickname he had picked up some eighteen years before at a quarter horse in Abilene. A stocky pinto thundering home on the quarter-mile run had unseated his rider, and the rider had been caught in one stirrup. The paint had lost its head and started to charge into a closely packed section of the spectators where there were women and children. Pa Burton—Sam Burton then—had plunged out and stopped the horse, partly by grabbing its loose reins but mostly by the sheer, crashing power of his own thick-set body.

"Jesus!" someone had yelled. "He stopped that calico like as if he was a stone wall!"

6

The name Stonewall had stuck.

A few weeks before, Pa had broken his leg when his saddle girth broke as he lassoed a maverick for branding. At fifty, when so many men who had built up their own cattle business were truly old men, Pa was as husky and wiry as a twenty-year-old. His leg had mended fast, and he was able to walk. He looked old, in a way. His hair was white and his fingers were gnarled. But, as he crossed in the evening shadows toward Clint, he still gave the impression of being a young mountain of a man.

Pa Burton stopped beside Clint and said, "What, son?"

"A rider. Kiowa, most likely. Pulled up on the crest of the hill behind the house. Then hightailed away."

Pa did not ask needless questions. Nothing like "What did he look like?" or "You're sure there was just one?" Sam Burton knew that his son had told him everything there was to say. He knew that the presence of one Indian might mean the existence of any number of them. A silent army could be hiding in the swelling folds of that steep hill, or even on the slightly undulating flat leading toward it. He knew that, considering his wife and second son, Pacer, it would be strange for a Kiowa not to visit the Burton place.

Pa Burton's eyes hardened with wary keenness as they searched the hill for a long moment, and then he went back into the house. The dim glow from the flames dancing up in the fireplace disappeared as battle shutters were quickly, quietly drawn over the windows and bolted.

Clint and Pacer finished the corral work before the setting sun had withdrawn all its light. There was a thin, half-evening light that cast no shadows as they went into the house and washed up.

"What was it?" Ma asked.

The three men sat at the table to wait for supper. Pacer, who had washed most recently, wiped a drop of water from his forehead where it was inching down from his ink-black hair. "Nothing. A rider. Some old hunter. Too spooky to come down and say hello."

Pa Burton glanced at his second son. It struck him as

7

strange that Pacer should be handier with words than Clint. Should be the other way around, he thought. Clint was older by five years, and it was Pacer who was half Indian. Maybe that was why Pacer could tell his mother a reassuring white lie so easily. Maybe that was why they had such a deep understanding of each other. If Sam or Clint had tried to tell Ma such a weak story, she would have known instantly, and she would have been doubly worried. But since Pacer had told her, she took it as the Gospel truth and was satisfied.

"Nothing so sad," she said, beginning to serve the pork and beans, "as an old man who has spent his life alone. After years of alone, it is hard to speak to another living creature."

Though she was satisfied with Pacer's explanation, Ma noted and marked it in her mind that each of the three men had his chosen gun close at hand. Clint, despite his training, had somehow forgotten to take off his revolver before sitting down to supper. Sam's buffalo gun was on the pegs over the fireplace only a step from his chair. Pacer had casually taken down his carbine "to clean it," although Ma was quite certain he had cleaned and oiled it only that morning, and he had not spoken of firing it during the day. The carbine leaned against the wall just behind him.

Ma noted these things but said nothing.

Their few words moved on now to quiet talk of the cattle they'd been hazing together for the spring roundup. Earlier that day Clint and Pacer had found nearly forty winter strays in a wide gully some twelve miles north. They had spent the afternoon driving the bawling, red-eyed longhorns to the sloping, grass-covered meadow about a mile east of the ranch, where the herd was slowly taking shape.

"I make it about six hundred head by now," Clint said.

Pa nodded. "Good. Might make 'er eight, nine hundred come trail time."

Across the table from Sam, Ma lifted her eyes suddenly to Sam's. Sam's fingers grew still on his coffee spoon.

"One horse," Pacer murmured as he moved swiftly

8

toward the closed and locked battle shutters, his carbine appearing suddenly in his hands.

"Maybe," Ma whispered, for it was habit to whisper on the rare occasions when an unknown person approached after dark. "Maybe the old hunter has come down from the hill."

CHAPTER TWO

Clint and Stonewall moved almost as swiftly as Pacer, each going to where he was most needed. Pa grabbed the tall, folding wooden shutters near the fireplace and pulled them across the front of the fire, so that the room was plunged into almost total darkness and therefore no light could show through cracks at the windows or door. Then, buffalo gun in hand, he hurried to the small window in the bedroom and squinted through a tiny crack out across the moonlit prairie. Pacer took a stand by the window in the main room. Clint was already at the front door. The three of them were so situated that they could see in any direction. The fourth wall, where the fireplace was, was more than two feet thick and stone-filled. It would be nearly impossible for anyone to get through there.

A husky, angry voice singsonged in the Kiowa tongue from the angle where Pacer watched. "Kee-nah-sote'ah. I am a Kiowa brother! I come in peace! Why do the small bits of light go out?"

Pacer, his dark eyes peering into the shadows where he could dimly make out the silhouette of the horseman, replied in fluent Kiowan, his voice as smooth and hard as a rifle barrel. "Why does a man who comes in peace wait until the sun is gone? Why does he stay hidden in the shadow of the moon?"

"The three of you, and the other, are alone?"

Listening intently, his revolver clutched ready in his hand and his eyes probing the shadowed landscape before the house, Clint once again found it strange, even absurd, that the Kiowas rarely used words for numbers larger than three. After three, it usually became simply "many," though this man was a clever speaker and had indirectly managed to give a clear idea of four.

Pacer handled the question adroitly and without hesitation. He also used the word "many."

"There are many of us in here." It could have been an admission of four, or a warning that there were twenty.

The angry-voiced Kiowa thought about this. Finally he said, "I am called Buffalo Horn. Buffalo Horn. My magic is very strong." He made a double play on the word "many" in turn now. "I lead many, many warriors. You have heard the name Buffalo Horn."

It was not a question but a statement. To say you had not heard of a warrior in his presence was a fighting insult. Pacer's flat answer was a thin cut this side of civility. "We have possibly heard of you. But we do not know many warriors who ride up on us in the dark."

"Warriors ride often in the dark."

"Then they are riding against their enemies. We are not the enemies of Kiowas." Pacer glanced across the darkened room toward Clint. He whispered, "Anything out front?"

"No." Another whisper. "Pa?"

Sam called softly to Clint, "Nothing moving here."

The man named Buffalo Horn was silent for a moment. Then he said in a voice somewhat less arrogant and angry, "It happens sometimes that there are people who are not enemies and who are not friends. That is what I have come to talk about."

Pacer followed up what seemed to be an advantage. "We have never been enemies with the Kiowas. To do that, we would have to be enemies with ourselves."

Buffalo Horn took this as a completely literal thought. "Are you enemies with yourselves?"

"No."

"Tell me this thing. Would you have fired upon us if I had come with many warriors?"

Pacer hesitated only a moment. "Yes."

"Good. You tell the truth. That is good. All good. Then I will no longer come with the dark. I will next come when the sun is in the sky." Buffalo Horn abruptly turned his

11

pony and rode away at a quick trot that turned into the sound of a lope before fading out of earshot.

After a long time, the men moved away from their lookout points, but they did not remove the shutter that hid the glow of the fire.

Pacer took a sip of coffee, not noticing that it had turned cold. "Funny kind of talk, that."

In the dark, Pa shrugged his heavy shoulders. "Could be he's some loco old coot. Wandering around, talking crazy, bragging about his magic. Sometimes it'll build up his medicine just on the grounds nobody knows what he's talking about."

Ma spoke then for the first time since the sound of hoofbeats had first come to their ears. In the deep shadows she looked toward Pacer and said in a motherly tone that was criticism couched in indulgence, "You said a hunter. He wasn't a hunter."

Clint could have told her she was wrong. He had got a good, long look at their visitor as he rode away from their house through a bright patch of moonlight. Buffalo Horn had been carrying a short war lance. Only the bravest fighters carried short war lances. To prove their courage and skill, they disdained the standard fourteen-foot weapon.

The war lance had carried at least seven scalps on it.

Buffalo Horn was a hunter.

CHAPTER THREE

Despite his stated opinion about "crazy talk," Old Stonewall had developed, over his twenty years on the plains, an instinctive feel toward a situation, and he was not often wrong. The simple proof of it was that he was still alive.

In the time of the Comanche trouble early in the Civil War, some of his neighbors had scoffed, "Good oak battle shutters are strong enough. Why lace 'em with iron stripping?"

Some of those neighbors were gone now—most of them dead. Without quite knowing why, acting by instinct, Pa had laced his battle shutters, and he'd stone-lined most of his thick walls, and his roof was interwoven with three to four feet of thick willows and hard-packed clay and mud. Partly this was for sheer strength of defense. But if Sam had bothered wondering beyond his instinct a little further, he would have found another reason deep in his brain. No one knew better than he how downright lazy the Plains Indians were. Though they could be bestial and savage at the height of a war raid, the very notion of chopping and hacking through heavy, tough walls was enough to make them sit down and talk things over. And they had always decided, evidently, that there was something better, after all, to do someplace else. This must be so, for they had never hit Sam's home, and the Comanches would just as soon take a Kiowa woman's scalp as a white woman's hair. Perhaps they'd even prefer it, since Ma was a pureblood Indian married to a white man, and a scalp with an interesting history made it twice as valuable.

13

It was this same instinctive reasoning that prompted Pa to speak to Clint after the morning chores were over, when they were all finishing breakfast. First light was trickling grayly into the house as he said, "Want you to ride to The Crossing."

"Fine."

"Not so fine." Old Stonewall's lips edged up into a faint, understanding grin. "No time for carryin' on with Roslyn Pierce. Expect you back by midnight."

The older man told Clint what he wanted, and Clint noted the list was heavy on shells. Pa finished by nodding at Pacer. "Take your brother along, Clint. Each of you take a pack horse. You'll make the forty mile easy by midnight."

Pacer said, "Pa, there's that thirty head or so Clint and me spotted off toward Buckskin Pass. Won't you need help bringing them in?"

"I'm strong enough to do it myself. So no, thanks, son."

When Pa said a thing politely, even though he really meant it to be pure friendliness, there was no further room for talk. It meant his mind was made up to a point beyond thinking about it, and he could relax and speak correctly, a habit he had gotten into when it occurred to him long ago that the boys would have to count almost entirely on him to learn their English.

Ma gave them some dried and flavorfully salted beef strips and a large piece of a cake she had baked to put in their saddle pockets. Clint put on the red shirt he wore for best, and they rode out, each with a lead horse on rein, before the sun had yet shown itself.

By common accord based on a simple exchange of glances, they did not ride straight for The Crossing. Instead, they swung at a slight angle and followed the hoofprints left by Buffalo Horn, now that it was light enough to see.

After half an hour of angling at a finger or two south of due east, they came to a place out of sight of their home, where Buffalo Horn had met other riders.

"Maybe twelve, fifteen of them," Pacer said. "Waiting for him while he rode in to talk to us."

14

Clint hooked his right leg up around his saddle horn while he took the time to build a smoke. Frowning, he ran his tongue over the edge of paper and then lit the cigarette. After slowly exhaling he said in a calm voice low-pitched with concern, "Did you notice? About every fifty feet or so—a drop of brown wet in the grass? I saw a few such spots. You make it what I do?"

Pacer nodded. "I saw. One of those scalps was fresh."

Sam had discovered a tiny patch of the dry, brown stains in the dust where Buffalo Horn had reined in his horse and had talked to them. He read the sign as his sons had. As Ma came out onto the porch into the flow of nearly horizontal warm gold cast by the rising sun, he shifted his game leg forward and scraped his boot back and forth to erase the faint marks on the ground.

Ma said, "Anything?"

Reflectively, Pa continued rubbing his boot for a moment longer in the dust. "No. Just kind of testing my leg. Not got much of the strength back in it yet, after all. Think maybe I'll take it easy for another day or so. Just work around the place here."

Perhaps in her pleasure at hearing it, Ma believed the story he had made up about his weak leg. "Good." She smiled. "Most of the time you don't have such good sense about caring for yourself."

Pleased about keeping his company, she went back into the house still smiling, and he knew that she was as yet unconcerned about the visit last night. This was probably because Buffalo Horn was one of her own people. Whatever the reason, the important thing was that she was still unafraid.

After twenty-two years of marriage, Sam felt that no man on earth could possibly know his own wife as well as he knew his. He understood her sometimes unreasoning fears, and he knew also the courage of which she was capable.

Her fears? Sam remembered the time when they had been married less than a month and had come to this place beyond the edge of civilization, this country border-

15

ing the Pecos Mountains and the land of the Wild Tribes in the west.

They had stopped one late afternoon at a bend in the Little Mississippi to water the horses. The bend was overcast by the shadow of a giant cottonwood which, Sam saw, had been struck by lightning years before. In the split trunk was wedged an Indian lance, charred by fire and gray with age. Sam had wondered if the lance had been driven into the tree before or after the lightning had struck. If before, it was a strange thing that the lance had not been completely destroyed by the lightning bolt. If the lance had been forced by a brave or a medicine man into the split after the bolt had struck the cottonwood, what had been the significance of burning a war lance? Either way, Sam had mused, it had seemed symbolic. He had decided then to settle here and to call his new spread Flaming Lance.

He had still been trying to call her by her Kiowa name then. It was N'edd'ee-pahs, and it meant Shining Star, or Star That Glows at Night. It had to be said, or sung actually, just so, or it meant nothing. For a while Sam had broken the name down to Nettie, but then, with the way she was taking care of little Clint—who was four and whose real mother had died on the trek west—the only name he could find right for her was Ma. Most Kiowa women were short, dumpy, dull-eyed creatures with harsh, hard voices and grating laughter. At seventeen Ma had been slim and sparkle-eyed, with a soft voice and gentle hands. She was still all those things, but age had stamped her in a hundred small ways: the white in her hair, the crow's-feet at the corners of her eyes, and the wrinkles in her forehead and in her fingers.

It was during that first month that Sam had first seen Nettie afraid. Toward the end of the day, she had come running into the half-built house which Sam was hammering solidly together.

Little Clint was clutched fiercely to her breast, and she cried, "Sam! Sam!" Her eyes were wide with horror, and Sam had been out of the door with cocked rifle in hands

16

about the same time his dropped hammer had hit the floor.

"What is it?"

"The small bird and the rabbit!"

"What?" Sam's eyes darted across the plain, sweeping the waving tall grass for signs of danger.

"The small bird and the rabbit!" she repeated in horror. "I saw them do the thing that was told me!"

After some minutes, he had quieted her down enough to explain. When she had been a child, a Kiowa medicine man had told the dream that he had had about her. If she ever saw a gray sparrow attack a rabbit, then someone she loved would die before the next setting of the sun. And now she had been walking along the tiny, nearby creek they called the Little Mississippi, a joke of Sam's that she did not understand. Suddenly she had heard a screeching of small-bird talk. Looking across the four-foot-wide Little Mississippi, she had seen a sparrow jabbering perhaps twenty feet away. A jackrabbit appeared and the sparrow, for no evident reason, flew straight at it. Instinctively, the rabbit had ducked, then thumped away as fast as it could go.

Ma was ill with fever all that night and all the next day, certain that Sam or Clint would die before the sun went down. She was so weak Sam had to carry her out to watch the setting sun and prove to her that the story was not true. She couldn't watch the sun go behind the range of the Pecos that formed Buckskin Pass, but instead she turned her face in on Sam's shoulder and wept silently. When the last of the sun's rays had disappeared behind the peaks, she was so grateful that Clint and Sam were still alive that she cried all over again.

Was the medicine false? Not at all, she'd told him. It simply meant that someone else who was dear to her had died before the sun went down. Chances were that she would never know whom the medicine had struck down.

Her courage? Sam would never forget the time two years later when he had been riding in from the slope to the east. He was perhaps a mile and a half away, able to

17

see but not close enough to help.

The infant Pacer had been put on a blanket in the yard so that he could play in the sun. From where Sam was, the blanket looked about the size of a fingernail and Pacer was but a dot on it. Ma was at the outside well with a bucket.

Sam had seen the bear first, and he had fired a shot into the air as a warning. Plenty of time to reload on the gallop in. As he pushed his horse into a streaking, desperate run, he tossed a slug into his mouth, ready to spit it into the barrel of his Hawken muzzle loader as soon as he'd poured powder into the big .60 muzzle.

It was a brown bear, an uncommon animal in this part of Texas. It had come lumbering in, silent as death, through the tall grass, and on its soft pads had jumped the Little Mississippi. Now, as Ma whirled and recognized the danger, the bear was only a few yards from Pacer. Ma rushed from the pump well, the half-filled bucket still in her hand, and ran swiftly to stand between her son and the bear. Without thought, she did the best thing she could. She waited until the advancing animal was close enough, then dashed the water from the bucket in its face.

The bear, surprised, grunted and whirled away, shaking its big, solid head. Then, turning back, it pushed up onto its hind paws and started toward the woman and her son. Sam was still too far away for a shot. His heart swelled in terror until he thought his chest would burst as he watched his wife facing up to the great beast towering above her. The only weapon she had now was the empty bucket, and she swung it in her hand like a club to fend off the bear. Shuffling awkwardly but fast, the beast grunted deep in its throat and swung a forepaw as powerful as an oak beam in a slashing arc that caught the bucket and whipped it rattling across the ground.

And then a big gun roared from inside the house. The bear was rocked off its feet and fell flat on its back. It turned twice on the ground, pawing at the air more and more feebly, until it died and lay still.

Six-year-old Clint had put a chair to the wall and had got the breech-loading Sharps down from its pegs. The

18

gun was longer than he was and weighed nearly half as much, but he had balanced the barrel over the window sill, cocked the gun, taken a long, careful aim, and pulled the trigger.

When Sam leaped from his still-moving horse, Ma had Pacer in her arms and was heading for the house. They found Clint and the Sharps stretched out together on the floor. When the boy started to sit up they could see that his jaw and shirt were covered with blood. The high hammer pull of the kicking Sharps had caught him in the mouth and ripped his lip open.

When they had stopped the bleeding and cleaned the wound with burning whisky, Sam, who did not let himself get carried away easily by his emotions, found his voice husky as he said, "Just a six-year-old boy."

Clint had grinned and then winched slightly as the grin tugged at his torn mouth. "Well, Pa, I doubt the bear was more'n six years old."

Sam hadn't taken the time to figure why he liked that statement. He just let it go that it made him proud. And still, looking back over the twenty years that had gone between, he found that the words somehow had a good ring to them.

But these thoughts now carried Sam back to his first thinking. He didn't believe anyone could possibly know Ma so well as he, yet perhaps Pacer did. There was an almost mystic bond between them, a strong cord of thoughts and feelings that stretched, invisible and unbreakable, from one to the other.

For all these years now Sam had had to fight a silent, running battle—a battle that was fought mostly with whispered words, veiled glances and cold silences—battle in which no gun had gone off, yet.

Their neighbors, the closest of whom lived seventeen miles away, could never be quite easy with Sam. They thought of him as a squaw man, though they never used such a name in the rare talks they had with him. Just once, back in '62 when the Kiowas and Comanches were raging over the lands east of the Staked Plains with hellish fury, a man had called him that to his face. Guns had almost gone off then. But Sam had put down his fierce hatred of the man enough to lay his gun down also.

Instead of shooting the man, he'd whipped him with his bare hands. When he had finished, they had sent the man to the hospital in Fort Worth. The man had never shown his face in this part of the country again.

No white man seemed able to understand that, to him, Ma was more than anything else a warm, loving woman, capable of the greatest kindness, the most intense loyalty, a woman who ran still and deep like a great river, yet who, like the bubbling currents in the river, loved to laugh.

Nor did the Indians understand her much better. To them, Ma was almost a rebel and a traitor. It bothered them little, because they thought about it little, but when N'edd'ee-pahs was spoken of around the cooking fires on the plains she was now referred to as "The-Thin-Woman-Who-Deserted-Her-People."

Couldn't a man and a woman fall in love? Couldn't it be that simple?

Riding across the immense reaches of the Texas plains for the first time, Sam had been a lonely and driven man—lonely within the grief of having, just two months before, lost Elizabeth to the fever that was striking travelers west, driven by his dreams of building a cattle empire, and driven by the fact that a small boy was grimly hanging to the saddle horn of the lead horse.

He never knew if he had found the Kiowas or if they had found him. But among the store of surprises the plains held for any man was the way these flats had of keeping people hidden until riders almost literally bumped into each other. He had ridden into a shallow wash and the three Kiowas had ridden around a bend in the wash not more than twenty feet away. Behind them, afoot, were four women. At first, talk was impossible. Sam did not even know the basic rudiments of intertribal sign language. He could sense that the Indians were considering attacking him, but they shied away from the idea. Sam Burton, even as a young and inexperienced man, was not the sort that three Kiowas were eager to fight without the element of surprise on their side.

The youngest woman had been called forward, and, with eyes lowered, she spoke a few halting words of English. "My . . . father . . . wish exchange . . . gifts." Briefly then she lifted her eyes and Sam was struck with almost physical force by the girl's resemblance to Elizabeth. A darker skin, jet-black hair, darker eyes. But the shape of the eyes, the set of the jaw could have made her Elizabeth's sister.

Sam had spent two days with the Kiowas and had ended up owning the girl in exchange for a Merwin & Hulbert that still shot pretty well and a pound of black powder. A month later, he had had a proper marriage and had settled along the Little Mississippi. His life was coming back into focus, becoming worth while and purposeful once more.

Ma's mother and father were long dead now, but she had seen them at least once a year while they lived. They would ride into the clearing between the Little Mississippi and the house, never choosing to come closer. Or a messenger might bring news of where they were and Ma would ride out to visit them. A sister of Ma's was still alive, and they saw each other once or twice a year. Ma had taken Clint with her at first when she went to the small village of her sister's husband. But Clint had early taken a dislike to the smells and sights of the Indian village. The first time he had seen them roasting a dog, the hair singeing off in the flames, he had gotten sick.

Ma had later taken Pacer with her. Pacer had picked up the difficult Kiowa tongue from her, and he took to speaking it easily. He saw her people in a different light from the way Clint did. He saw the freedom of movement over the plains as opposed to the solitary, stationary imprisonment of a solid house. He saw more beauty than Clint did in a beautifully woven porcupine-quill vest or a splendidly wrapped and colored war lance.

Perhaps it was because Pacer's blood was half Kiowa. Sam didn't pretend to know, and, what was more important, he didn't care. He viewed his sons evenly. Good men. Strong men. Loyal men. That was all he asked.

And beyond asking, he fervently hoped that his sons would manage to make full and worthwhile lives for them-

21

selves on the raw, rugged frontier he had grown to love.

But would they be able to do so with the brand of Kiowa blood on the family? A carefully closed door in Pa Burton's mind opened briefly. Clint and Pacer were grown men now. And to Pa's mind there had been a purposefulness, maybe a threat of war, in Buffalo Horn's visit. Whether this was simply bad thinking, or whether they would actually come to the savage reality of shedding blood, the thinking had reopened the door in Pa's mind and caused him to ask the question he had asked himself so often before.

Tempers and emotions flared quickly, violently, here on the frontier facing the Wild Tribes. If it came to war, Clint and Pacer, the entire Burton family, would be distrusted by both whites and Indians.

No matter how strong they were, with their background, would his sons, the future of Flaming Lance, be able to survive?

CHAPTER FOUR

Riding at the best speed possible without overtiring their mounts, Clint and Pacer spoke once more on the tiring, twenty-mile ride. This was while, by the silent, common accord in which they habitually worked and lived together they had stopped to water the horses at a shallow, barely moving stream.

Pacer's hands, slenderer and darker than Clint's but almost as strong, were idly pulling a few snarls from his horse's mane while his restless eyes studied the broad land around him. "Why'd Pa want me to come?"

"One man can hold the house. For a while. Two men have a less chancy time in the open."

"Buffalo Horn's a Kiowa. Kiowas wouldn't hit our place."

"Maybe."

Pacer glanced at his brother with a brief, wondering look. "You think they would?"

Pulling up the head of his lead mare, who was drinking too deeply, Clint said, "I guess a man's a notch safer if he figures most anything might happen."

They found The Crossing deserted when they rode in that afternoon.

The Crossing was one general store, a blacksmith shop and two houses. In ten years it might be gone, except for sagging roofs and broken windows and memories. Or in the same ten years it might sprout some other buildings and be on its way to becoming a regular town. Its fate would depend on cattlemen, advancing railheads and Indians, any one of which could knock it out of business by doing the wrong thing at the wrong time. The Crossing had survived one large Indian attack, as well as the coming of a railroad to Fort Worth, in its ten years' existence. Except for a few cattle drives to those small cow towns called Fort Worth and Wichita, which overwhelmed both Clint and Pacer with their noise and their sour-oil-and-sawdust smells, this was the closest they'd ever come to civilization.

The Pierces owned the general store, or rather Dred Pierce did. His wife had died long ago—some said worked to death—and Dred now ran the store with the help of his daughter, Roslyn. His son, Angus, a thick-set hulk of a man, had long since been hired out to Ben Ford, who ran the blacksmith shop. There was more profit for Dred that way.

Dr. Phillips, who was good with both livestock and human beings, lived in one of the two nearby houses with his family—wife, three sons and a small girl. The other house was occupied by old Homer Jensen, his wife and two sons. Homer, they said, had struck it rich in Deadwood in the rush of '76. He did no work, but he always had enough to pay for whisky at the bar in Pierce's General Store, where he spent most of his time. They said Homer hated people, and he hated loneliness, and this was as close as he could get to doing away with both.

Approaching the lonely town, and thinking of the rust-brown spots along Buffalo Horn's trail. Clint felt the hair at the back of his neck rising slightly. "Wonder where everybody is?"

Pacer shook his head, and Clint knew his brother had the same spooky feeling. "Crossing hasn't been hit. No damage."

They rode into the deserted space between the two houses and the two places of business that passed as a street. They pulled up silently in front of the store and, after hitching their horses, went into the building.

No one was in the big, main room that was crowded and stacked with canned goods, saddlery, plows, tools and every other thing that a west Texan might conceivably

24

want to buy. Pacer noticed a fancy, silver-worked bridle toward the rear of the store that must have come in on a freighter since their last trip to The Crossing nearly two months before. Curious, but walking cautiously, he went back to examine it.

Clint waited in the center of the large room for a long, silent moment. Then he called in a mild but carrying voice, "Anybody around here?"

There was the thud of heavy footsteps, and Angus Pierce strode into the room through the back door. He was dressed in his leather blacksmith apron but was naked from the waist up. The corded muscles that bulged from his heavy arms to his thick neck were tense and beaded with sweat. His eyes were haggard, but they blazed with the fire of a sudden decision when he saw Clint. "You!" He hesitated beyond where Pacer stood silently holding the bridle near the wall, and with his eyes boring at Clint he did not see Pacer at all.

"Yes," Clint said softly, sensing the savage undertone of hostility behind Angus' words, but not understanding it. "It's me."

"You!" Angus almost roared the word. "I been doin' a lotta thinkin' about you."

Clint knew that Angus was neither smart nor even-tempered, but he had never seen such hatred in a man's eyes and the most terrible part of it was that Angus was making a mighty effort not to show it, trying so hard to keep his booming voice calm that it nearly cracked under the strain. Clint waited.

Angus stood silent for a moment, licking his lips. Suddenly, like a man forcing himself to do something in direct contrast to his will, he walked stolidly toward Clint and put out his hand. "I'm your friend, Clint! I want to shake hands with you."

Wondering, Clint put out his own hand, and Angus' big, hairy paw settled around it.

And then Angus said something that could have caused him to die in the next moment.

"I'm your friend," he grated in a voice torn with emo-

25

tion. "We've always been friends. But if he ever sets foot in this store again, I'll—kill that brother of yours! The dirty breed!"

The bridle Pacer was holding fell to the floor with a faint thump.

Clint's face grew white under his deep tan and he tightened his grip on the other's hand. In a low voice edged with fury, he said, "I won't strike you, Angus."

And then every weight of power in Clint's wide, leather-tough body went surging into the grip he had on the other man's hand.

Angus grunted in pain and for an instant tried to answer the cruel force crushing his hand. His grunt turned to a low cry of agony, and he fell forward on one knee, reaching blindly for Clint's wrist with his free hand.

Releasing his hold, Clint stepped one pace away from where Angus was kneeling. He whispered, "Shaking hands was a mistake for both of us."

Angus was dimly aware that something had fallen behind him. Turning and seeing Pacer, he shouted, "Get out! I'll kill you if you set foot here again! I won't sell you nothin'!" Then, with a cry of rage, he got up and, with his right hand still useless, started to where old Dred Pierce kept a shotgun behind the bar.

Clint swept his revolver up out of its belt holster and the hammer clicked back. "Touch that and I'll kill you, Angus."

Angus whirled around, but before he could frame an answer in his mind, a girl's commanding voice came from the stairs leading to the second floor. "Don't touch it, Angus. He means it."

Clint glanced at Roslyn Pierce, the girl he had learned to know so well over the past two years, and he saw that her face was as hard and pale as ice.

"All right," she said, making an effort to control her voice. "You've shown how strong you are. Now will you have the decency to take your brother and get out?"

Clint managed to keep his tone level. "Have you both gone crazy?"

"No," she told him, her eyes glazed with the emotion

26

she tried to keep out of her words, "we're not crazy. Just smarter than before."

"But what—"

"The Kiowas hit the Howard place last night. And do you know what's left out of a family of five?" Her voice trembled now, on the verge of tears. "Oh, of course, there were some lumps of charred meat in what was left of the house. But that could be beef, or it could be human. All that's left to recognize is one human hand!" She hesitated, then added, "We think it . . . Dorothy—"

"Don't!" Angus pleaded, but his sister went on.

"Before the hand had been chopped off, the fingers had been split down the middle." She paused. "That means she'd been taken alive—"

"Stop!" Angus bellowed. "Stop it!" He bolted and ran out of the back door toward the blacksmith shop.

"He's making a coffin for her now!" Roslyn's voice edged closer to a sob. "What size should you make a coffin when all you've got to bury is a hand?"

Clint's gun hung limply at his side. He knew that Angus and Dorothy Howard had planned to be married in the fall. His shock and horror made it hopeless to say the right words. "Is there," he stammered, "anything—anything we can do?"

"Our men are out chasing the Kiowas, and the last they tracked of them, they were heading toward your place. But they're your friends," she continued. "You don't look like you've been in much of a battle!" The high, ragged edges of the girl's voice were getting away from her. She turned and ran quickly back up the stairs.

Pacer had still not moved. Now he crossed to Clint. His feelings were too strained for normal talking. He whispered, "Let's go."

But sheer, rugged stubbornness welled up in Clint and he said, "We will. But we came for some things. We're not leaving without them."

They knew the store almost as well as the Pierces did. They found the supplies they needed, left some money, and within a few minutes were on their horses riding out of The Crossing.

27

Only once did they speak on the twenty-mile ride back. When the sun was low on the Pecos far to the west, Clint touched Pacer on the shoulder. His fingers rested gently but firmly on his brother's shoulder for a moment, and then he withdrew his hand. "They're out of their heads," he muttered. "In time they'll come to their senses."

A long time later, almost as though hearing Clint for the first time now, Pacer shook his head. "I can never—never go back to that place again."

Most of the things that Clint could think of to say seemed wrong, so he said nothing except "It's only twelve miles farther ride to the trading post at The Fork. We can trade there."

And then they were at the ten-mile point from home and began to push their mounts into a long, fast clip that would exhaust but not ruin them over a ten-mile distance. It was darkening now.

Pa might be needing help.

CHAPTER FIVE

Ma Burton's hand moved patiently up and down in a practiced gesture as she dipped the last of the candles. Each time the slender-coated wick descended into the liquid hot tallow another coating of the fat cooled and clung to the slender cylinder, making the candle a little fatter. When this candle was finished there would be enough tallow left to mix with a handful of powdered ashes to make two or three bars of soap.

Her eyes moved to the cooking board where seven already dipped candles were lined and hardening in a row, and Ma realized for maybe the thousandth time how much she loved the word "candle."

"Candle" sounded so right for what it was. The first part of the word started off like the sound of "dance," and then it finished up soft and gentle, coming from deeper in the throat where sounds of love and beauty were made. Ma could not look at the soft waving flow of yellow light tipping a candle without thinking of the flame as a gentle dancer.

The sounds of words had intrigued Ma since very early in her life when she had been Star That Glows at Night, of the Men'ote-tsah people, a poor village of perhaps forty men, women and children. The night she had been born, two things had happened out of the ordinary. Her mother had told her that all through her birth a wild dog had sat on a nearby hill and barked. Ma still felt a faint shudder at the fact that she had very nearly been named Barking Dog. But someone had noticed a new star in the sky, a star that shone with a brightness that had not been seen before.

Ma had been sixteen when the long-beard dressed in

black had visited her village. He had no horse, and nothing else worth stealing, so the men had let him live. He had tried to teach those who were interested a strange and exciting new language. Ma had picked up new words as a child picks up pretty pebbles, with happy fascination. At first she had thought this new tongue was the Bible language, for that was the word the long-beard used most. Over the summer he had spent with them, she and she alone had picked up a smattering of English. Oddly, the words he had tried hardest to teach her were the words she disliked most: God. Christ. They sounded harsh on her ear, like fighting words, and when he spoke them there came a wildness into his eyes and voice that frightened her.

He had gone his way with the first chill of early winter, leaving the young Indian girl with a fear of God that never allowed her to embrace Him. To this day, Ma pictured the Christian God as a giant man with wild eyes whose wrath it was the simplest thing in the world to incur. Hell-fire and brimstone, with angry flames eating you up. This is what the wicked person could expect from a Christian death, and the long-beard had said that all men were wicked. It was better to keep the Kiowan gods. If one of them turned against you, you would still have a chance of finding protection with one or more of the others. Ma preferred the Kiowas' idea of death. An old, old legend, passed down through the generations, said that if you saw a black star in the sky, death would come soon to you. It gave you warning; you could prepare yourself for what lay ahead. The Kiowas called it the Black Star of Death.

When Sam had appeared, almost magically, the girl's immediate family were about to make a trip to another Kiowan tribe in an effort to sell her before she became too old to be any good to anyone. The way he'd appeared suddenly before them, sitting tall and straight and mighty in the saddle, her father and brothers had speculated on whether he had some potent magic power.

No man had offered to buy her at her late age of seventeen summers because she was too weak-looking, too thin. Her father had been delighted when Sam offered him a gun for her, but the shrewd old man had sold six daughters, and he concealed his delight long enough to hold out for a pound of black powder also.

When Ma had first looked at Sam she had seen, as the others had, an almost metallic hardness to his eyes. But she had looked deeper, and she had seen a great hurt, a great need, and a great capacity for kindness.

Somehow his eyes reminded her of the warrior whom the Kiowas considered the finest war chief of all time. The young Chiricahua Apache, Goyathlay, had visited her tribe many years before, looking for warriors to go south to fight the Mexicans. Goyathlay had just lost his woman, his mother and three sons when the Mexican horse soldiers attacked an unarmed Apache camp bent on peaceful trade. Something in the underlying sorrow filling Sam's eyes, something in the suggestion of fearful power in his relaxed but ready body brought to mind this chief, who was now known by the name of Geronimo.

Ma had been so happy at being bought by Sam that she wept silent tears where she lay alone that first night, and did not sleep. He had done no more than touch her hand until they had visited another black-suited man to the north who read to them from a book and told them they were man and wife.

Then they had come to the Little Mississippi, and Ma's life had been richer, fuller than she had ever hoped or dreamed it might be. There were Sam and young Clint, and, later, Pacer.

Two fine sons and a good husband. What woman on this earth could ask for more?

Sam had built the walls of his home strong, to protect her. But Ma sometimes thought of herself standing out on the open, sweeping land with no building in sight. She pictured her three men around her, if danger threatened. And she knew that nowhere—nowhere could anyone find stronger walls than these men.

If, after all these years, it was still impossible to go to The Crossing or any place where white people gathered; if it was impossible not to feel the withdrawal of the other settlers on the rare occasions when she saw them, that was all right. It was all right because Ma had all she needed.

Her only concern was for Pacer and Clint. Even by the lonely standards of the plains, their lives had been lonely and friendless. It concerned Ma more and more now that they were full-grown men who should be thinking of marrying and starting their own families.

Ma judged the candle to be the right size now and she stopped dipping, holding it up by the wick to let the first dryness set it before lining it up on the cooking board with the others.

Sam limped in with an armload of wood and an extra bucket of water. He had busied himself around the house with small chores, catching up with work that would not take him far from the house. And now the extra bucket of water. There was only one reason for the additional water. There was enough already for normal drinking, cooking and washing. This was for an emergency, for the easing of a long thirst, or for the cleansing of wounds.

Ma turned from where she was starting the evening meal. "You can't believe they would come down on us, Sam?"

After placing the filled bucket under the cooking board, Sam put the sawed wood neatly in its place near the fire. "Something bad is on the wind."

"But Lame Crow is a strong chief. He wouldn't let them. They'd be afraid . . ."

Sam Burton had his own feelings about Indian names. Lame Crow, the husband of Ma's sister, had always claimed to be a powerful leader, but Sam believed that a strong man would have changed his name if he had had a worth-while battle or reputation to found a new name on. Besides, if there was trouble, the Kiowas would be only half of their danger.

"We won't be attacked," Ma said, trying to smile to Sam the assurance that was in her. And then, looking at his set face, she suddenly realized what he was thinking. "No, Sam," she murmured. "No. The whites wouldn't attack us! They wouldn't harm you!"

Sam said nothing. He guessed that Ma would know that no man could hurt him except through her.

The dark was coming fast now, and he closed the battle shutters.

Clint and Pacer arrived at Flaming Lance two hours before midnight. Clint gave a low whistle from the corral so that Ma and Pa would know who was out in the night. He and Pacer took care of the horses and carried the supplies up to the house. At their first step on the porch the door swung open. They entered and Pa closed and bolted it behind them.

Both of the young Burtons looked tired, more tired than a week's riding should have made them.

While Ma ladled supper for them, Pa said, "What's wrong?"

"The Howard place got hit." Clint put the supplies he carried on the table and tossed his hat wearily onto his bunk standing against the wall. "Massacre."

Ma stopped in her ladling and the hand holding the big spoon trembled for a brief moment. "Kiowa?"

"Yes, Ma."

Her face tightened into deep, hollow lines of sorrow. "Oh, the poor, poor Howards."

Pacer said flatly, "They'd like to died four years ago if you hadn't gone over to tend them through the fevers. Way I see it, you gave them four years' extra life." He finished almost angrily, "They were lucky for that."

"Pacer, what a terrible thing to say!"

"Buffalo Horn?" Pa asked, his voice casual. It was a way of Sam's thinking to fret about a thing before it came to pass. But once it was upon them, as this now was, he was as cool as a root cellar.

"Most like." Clint spoke for himself and Pacer, though they had never exchanged thoughts on the subject during the ride. They didn't have to. He added with a shade of discomfort, "We didn't learn too much about the raid. Came back in a hurry."

Sam glanced at his eldest son keenly. "Did you learn what there was to learn?"

"No."

Stonewall Burton's face took on the hard glint of a

33

living rock for which he had gotten his nickname and he moved his eyes from one son to the other, ignoring the food that had been placed before him. He said, "I understand."

Without looking up from where she was banking the fire, Ma said simply, "We all understand, Sam." She stood up, wiping her hands on her apron. "It's my fault for being what I am."

"I speak for the three of us," Sam said slowly. "We do not want to hear such a thing said—ever again."

Ma nodded slowly, silently. She turned and walked to the cooking board, standing motionless with her back to them, her head bowed.

Crossing to her, Sam put a big hand softly on her back. "You hear this, Nettie." He still called her that sometimes, when his mind was turbulent and she seemed to him to be the young girl he had first married. "Whatever happens, it will be with us as it has always been. This family will stick together and we will not be swayed. If we have to live alone on the face of the earth, if we have to become a power unto ourselves, we'll resist whatever, whoever comes against us."

CHAPTER SIX

Clint could not sleep. He lay in his bunk. He could hear
Pacer's almost soundless, regular breathing in the bunk
below him. He did not think Pacer was asleep either, but
it was impossible to tell with his younger brother. Pacer
slept so lightly that the faintest noise or foreign movement
woke him instantly and completely. So that now, if Clint
were to whisper a word, Pacer would answer immediately,
and it would be anyone's guess whether he'd been sleeping
or simply lying with his eyes closed.

Clint's thoughts went out into the dark room to touch
the things he knew so well in that small space. Though he
could not understand why, every object in the room was
dear to him just now, and thinking on them brought a
faint, bittersweet pain to his chest. Only a few inches from
his head was his nickel-plated, walnut-handled Frontier
Colt .41, which hung in its holster from the bunk. Of all
his possessions, Clint treasured this most. Pa had given it
to him ten years ago, the last year they'd driven stock up
to Wichita and the first year Clint had been judged man
enough to pull his own weight on a cattle drive.

Pa had paid off the four temporary hands who had
helped take the five-hundred-head herd up the Shawnee
Trail. Then Pa and Clint had wandered through the small,
wild cow town. Clint had seen the beautifully designed
revolver, which was still new on the market, in a
hardware-store window—and Pa's eyes had followed his.

"I will not pay my son wages," Pa had said as they
looked at the fine gun. "What I have is my son's as well,
and it wouldn't be fitting to pay you out of money that is
as much yours as mine. But perhaps you would like to

spend some of our money to buy that weapon?"

"I'd like that, Pa."

The revolver had been stocked in .38, .41, .44, and .45 calibers. Clint didn't know which to take. Pa had suggested the .41. "It's a gentleman's gun. It will do as good a job anytime, without the loud boom and pretense of the larger bores."

Later, when they had hooked onto the Shawnee Trail headed south, Pa had said thoughtfully, "The gun has the look of being at home on your side, Clint. Leave it there, always, if you can take care of yourself in any other way."

In ten years Clint had never pointed the Colt at a man—until today.

But he did not want to think about today, and his mind moved on to other things in the room, trying to skirt the incident at The Crossing. There was the table in the center of the room that Pa had made during a snow-in. The first one they had had was a cheap, store-bought square table that had groaned under the considerable weights a lone table had to take in a ranch-house. This one was oval, with four strong, handsomely carved legs, and its oak top could have supported a stomping steer.

Six years before Pacer, Roslyn and he had played maybe a hundred games of checkers on that table. When Angus had caught the mumps late and the Pierces were afraid Roslyn might come down too, they'd sent her to the Burtons for the waiting time. Clint tried to go on to other things, but his mind had been caught by Roslyn and wouldn't leave her.

The burning fireplace behind her back had glowingly framed her pale-yellow hair, so that it had looked very like the picture of a saint Clint had seen in a book. Very like a halo. She had been fifteen at the time, slender and wiry and in some ways almost boyish, but already enough aware of the woman in her not to be a saint at all. Clint had been bothered by his thoughts about her, thoughts he was pretty sure she could see in his eyes, so he'd said a thing to make it light. "Roslyn, have you ever considered that we could all retire and go live in Kansas City if we had a dollar for every freckle on your face?"

Her answer had been to up-end the checker-board into his lap, spilling the checkers every which way. "Oh, you're so funny!" Then she'd marched past him out in the dusk to the corral.

Pacer had said, "Clint, you hurt her feelings."

"Oh, the hell."

They were picking up the checkers when Ma came in with some fresh laundry. "Something wrong. Roslyn said she's going out to look at the horses. She's seen horses before."

Clint had glanced at Pacer under the table. "You really think that?"

"Yeah."

So he'd gone out and walked up behind Roslyn and found her crying, her arms folded over the top rail. "Roslyn, honest. Freckles or not, I think you're the prettiest girl around here."

"Oh, fine!" She'd dried her tears quickly and indignantly. "There's maybe ten girls in a thousand miles around here."

"Yes, but—you know what I mean."

After a little she'd said, "I'm sorry I ruined the game. We'll count it for you. You were winning."

"Let's play another game to decide."

And it had grown, as Roslyn grew, from a friendship to something closer, and finally, in the last two years, into a more or less understood feeling of marriage.

Clint wondered why he'd held back. His best guess was that there had always been the flavor in the air of what had turned so bitter today. The few folks who knew Ma gave her up to be a pure queen of a woman. Anybody who didn't respect and admire Pacer was out of his mind. Yet there was bad feeling; or if there was acceptance, it was somehow made clear that the very acceptance was proof of broad-mindedness and generosity. And Clint could tolerate neither.

Pacer moved in the bunk below, shifting his legs onto the floor. He had a boot in his hand as Clint came down

37

from the top bunk, silently and swiftly. They had heard the faint, shuffling sound simultaneously. Walking horses. Several of them.

They had their boots on and Clint was buckling on his gun in the dark when the bedroom door opened and Sam came into the room in his stockinged feet.

Peering through a battle-shutter crack, Clint gazed out into the moon-spilled whiteness of land before the house. "Whites," he said softly. "I make it eight of them."

The dark-gray silhouettes of horsemen pulled up a short stone's throw from the house, and a loud voice called, "Clint! Clint Burton!"

"That's Dred Pierce," Sam said.

"I'll go talk to them." Clint shot the bolt on the door and stepped out, beyond the porch and into the moonlight. "What you want, Dred?"

Now that he was in sight, the horsemen came slowly closer until he could make out their faces. Besides Dred, there was Ben Ford, the blacksmith, who was so big he looked as though he could get off and carry his horse. There was Howie Jensen, two of the Holcum boys, and three men from the big Cannon family, who had the Flying Bucket, the largest ranch in the area.

"Want to talk to you, Clint," Dred said too casually.

"Talk."

Pierce's voice was unnatural in its easiness. Here was a man who was a born complainer, a thin, dust-dry man who carried eternal worries on his slightly stooped back, and he was talking for the first time in Clint's memory as though he were discussing the weather on a pleasant afternoon.

"Been chasin' the Kiowa," he began. "Lost 'em out west of Banner Pass." He hesitated. "They murdered the Howard family."

"We heard."

"Oh?" Dred didn't ask how. "The Howards was a fine family. This has broke all of us up. M' boy Angus is near out of his head. The Kiowa come close t' your place at one time. They're bein' headed up by a brave name of Buffalo Horn."

38

"They know all that," Ike Holcum said, his voice savagely flat and impatient. "Buffalo Horn like as not stopped by t' brag on what he done."

Clint shifted his feet slightly so that he faced Holcum squarely. "Ike, I'll not hear another word like that."

Holcum grunted, "Well, git to it, Pierce."

"You shut up!" Dred told him, trying to keep his strained voice conversational. "I'm doin' our talking! Thing is, Clint, this particular Indian can cause us more trouble than we ever saw before. Unless he gits stopped. He made a strong medicine up north a while back. Made some kinda liquid that his warriors rubbed on their skin t' protect them from bullets. Make slugs bounce off 'em like raindrops. They got in a fair-sized skirmish with a lotta shootin', and not one of his boys got so much as scratched. So that makes him a big man. What helps him even more, he's got but one eye, like that big medicine man from way up northeast back in '28. A witch doctor they called the Prophet. Tecumseh's brother. Kiowas 're impressed as hell with him, and young warriors are supposed t' be coming from all over to join up with 'im."

Clint nodded. "So?"

"So, we been doin' some talking about you." The strain of sounding calm was edging sharply now into Dred's voice. "We like you, boy. We'd like t' know if you're with us."

"Though we wouldn't trust anybody else in your red-lovin' family as far's we could spit," Holcum tossed in.

Clint's hand moved swiftly toward the gun at his side as rage flashed through his mind, and the men on horseback reached quickly for their own weapons.

"Hold!" Sam's voice exploded from the porch behind Clint. "First man takes a gun out gets a buffalo slug in him!"

Clint did not know how long Sam and Pacer had been standing there in the dark of the porch, backing him. His hand trembling, he let his Colt drop back into its holster.

"Take two steps back, son," Sam told him.

When this was done, Sam and Pacer moved up to stand beside him, and they were all three in the shadows. The ominously huge barrel on Pa's buffalo gun jutted into the milky moonlight like a cannon sticking out of a redoubt. Pacer held his carbine ready.

"Dred," Sam said softly, "do you think the Howards meant nothing to us?"

Dred shifted uncomfortably in his saddle, staring at the big-barreled gun. "Not the question, Sam."

"Then what is the question?"

"It's one of . . . loyalty, you might say."

"Keep talking."

"We—well, damnation, Sam! Your wife is a Kiowa. Pacer there's half Indian blood. You ain't never been hurt none by redskins."

"I built a strong house."

"Sure, but any fool can see it ain't with you like it is with us. Far as we're concerned, Clint's the only real white man in the family. So's it seemed fair to give him his chance t' be loyal to his own kind, to see how he stood."

There was a long silence, and then the steady barrel of the buffalo gun shook slightly and Sam, almost inaudibly, let out his pent-up breath. "Clint, it might be good for you to weigh what Dred says. Maybe I haven't been fair to anyone in my family to have brought us to this pass. If you ride away with these men, you might be happier for it in the long run—and you'd do so with my blessing."

"The only move I'll make," Clint said quickly, "is to shoot Ike Holcum next time he opens his mouth."

"May I say something?" Sam asked Dred, the unwavering gun barrel silently guaranteeing this privilege. "We've lived in peace, us Burtons, for a long time. But we have always been ready and able to fight. I say to you that Buffalo Horn is my enemy for what has been done to the Howards. Just as white murderers or bandits would be my enemy because of their crimes. And we are prepared, if need be, to fight any men who prove to be our enemies."

"You by chance includin' us?" Ben Ford grunted.

"That depends on you, Ben. We're equally prepared to be friends with those who prove worthy of friendship. It's that simple. Your visit tonight has not been friendly."

"How'n hell can it be?" Ike Holcum demanded. "When

waitin' on you inside you got a Kiowa squaw!"

The buffalo gun and Pacer's carbine swung toward Ike, but it was Clint's revolver that roared. He'd taken it out as Ike began to talk, and he fired on Ike's last word. Holcum was shoulder-hit and sent spinning off his horse to land face down on the ground.

Dred raised both hands and shouted, "Don't shoot!" so that no one ever really knew whether he was talking to the Burtons or, as he later claimed, to his own men to avoid more bloodshed. The mounted men hesitated at his yell, realized that three guns in the shadows were bad odds, and did not fight. Ike Holcum struggled to his knees, one hand clutching his bleeding shoulder, and muttered, "Oh, my God, my God! I'm shot! I'm bad hurt!"

"You're lucky you're alive," Pacer said quietly. "I'd have killed you."

Knees wavering, Ike got to his feet and his brother Joe helped haul him back up into the saddle of his nervous mare.

"I'm sorry it's come to this," Sam said.

"You ain't heard your last from us," Ben Ford told him, turning his horse. "Not by a long shot."

Ma's voice came from the doorway, firm and clear. "Bring that man in here. He needs looking after."

Joe Holcum paused, with one hand helping to steady Ike, not knowing what to do. Ike shrugged away angrily, almost throwing himself again. "I wouldn't . . ." He did not finish, but turned his horse with knee pressure and clucked it into a walk.

Hanging back as the others rode away, Dred looked into the shadows where Clint stood. "I'll tell Roslyn we give you your chance. And you chose t' throw it away."

"I guess she already knows."

Pierce trotted after the others, and after they'd ranged out of sight and sound, Sam lowered his big gun. "Thank God you didn't kill him, Clint."

Wiping his forehead with the back of his hand, Clint found a blanket of sweat there. "Something inside made me pull off. Not easy to kill a man."

They went inside to where Ma had started to heat some

coffee. "They should have let me tend him," she murmured, tightening her house dress against the cool of night that the small fire had not yet pushed away. "They ought not have let him act so foolish." She went to where Clint was standing by the table and touched his cheek gently. "Sit down, Clint. Hot coffee will make you feel better."

There were several shots in the distance, then a low murmur of rolling sound. Sam reached for his gun where he had leaned it near him, but changed his mind. "Might as well have that coffee. Can't do any good now."

Pacer's carbine was clutched in hands stiff with angry tension. "Let me go, Pa! I can get a couple of them!"

"No." The older man shook his head. "We'd be too few out there. And the harm is already done."

Ma frowned, disbelieving. "Are they stampeding our herd?"

"Yes." Pa nodded wearily. "Running them south into the broken country. Be a job, rounding them up down there."

Pacer's face was so tight the muscles in his jaw stood out in clear separation. "A little parting gift from our white friends."

CHAPTER SEVEN

Come the first plum-colored light of day, Sam and Clint took saddles from the leather shed and made ready to ride out. The first day's work would be the most important, and Clint was the best man with cattle in the Burton family. Therefore, Pacer was left to work around the house and to be on guard.

The longer the steers roamed free, the better chance they had to be lost. Normally, had stock mavericked off onto another range, the cowman who wound up with them would pay Sam off, less driving charges, after the next drive to a railhead. But Sam guessed that cows lost to him now would be lost forever, that the interrange agreement no longer included him. Only thing to do was to get back every one of his Flaming Lance-brand animals that he could.

The two men were still in sight of the distant speck of a house when they cantered to the crest of a hill and Clint pulled in his patch pony. Tonelessly he said, "There's the first of our herd."

Sam looked through the graying dawn, and the muscles in his flat stomach tightened. Piled in a steep draw were about twenty steers. In the night run, they had plunged over the bank and piled up until they had made a slanting runway of flesh for the other animals to run over. The upside of the broken pile of flesh and bones was a trampled level of blood and hoof-cut hides. On a small ranch such as Sam's, it wouldn't take many more dead steers to make the difference between existence and go-broke.

Again with no tone one way or the other, Clint spoke. "I should have killed Holcum."

"No, son. You did right."

"We should've cut them all down. They're worse than Indians. An Indian'll rob you blind if he can. But this was plain waste and meanness."

They pushed on across an oak-brush flat two miles wide, where the short, tough branches and trunks of the brush had been ripped and torn along a broad front by the panicked herd. They passed three more dead steers on the flat. At the far edge the land broke up into rough country filled with ancient and now dry stream-cut gullies and wind-eroded hills. Here the herd had split in numerous directions.

"I believe most of the run was taken out of them by the time they got here," Sam said.

That first day they gathered about a hundred and fifty head, after combing every draw, gully and hollow in nearly a hundred square miles. It was Clint's idea to herd them into Elder Box Canyon. Grass was not so good there, but for that very reason it would be an unlikely place for marauders to look.

They got home well after midnight, and by first light the next morning they were in the saddle once more, this time taking lead horses because they would be riding out even farther, covering too much distance for one cutting pony to carry a man's weight.

Pacer watched them go. He'd offered to switch with Clint or Sam, but they claimed, rightly, that they knew the ground they'd covered and could work more efficiently without retracing themselves too much in the badlands.

This was the day that Buffalo Horn, as he had promised, came back in the light of the sun.

Pacer's nerves were, as much as was possible for a strong and quiet man, on edge. He finished feeding corn to the four horses that were to be used the next day, beefing them up for the killing work that would be expected of them. Then he turned to look once again at the faraway Pecos Mountains where they formed Buckskin Pass. Earlier that day, he had seen something that he neither understood nor liked. It was so far away that most eyes would never have caught it. A moving speck so tiny as to be almost invisible had appeared near the summit of the cliff forming the south wall of Buckskin Pass. Pacer had squinted keenly, and it had seemed to him that what he was looking at was a man on foot—a wild man who waved his arms senselessly as he stumbled blindly a few steps before disappearing among the rugged rocks lining the cliff.

It had been such a brief, fleeting impression that Pacer wasn't sure whether it had happened in his eyes or in his mind. And if it had been in his mind, then it must have been a sign. But a sign of what? The thought of swinging up on a pony bareback and riding to that distant place came to Pacer but was instantly rejected. It would be too far to go, leaving Ma alone at the house.

That it was necessary for him to be here at all, with so much work to be done in the badlands, brought a ragged, black cloud of rage into Pacer's thinking. That his mother should be in danger from anyone at anytime, being the woman she was, was unthinkable to him.

Yet it had always been so. Pacer's first memory was more of a dream than a true remembrance. It was of a wide, clear sky stretching endlessly over him. Into this serenity had come a lumbering, snuffling danger that Pacer had not recognized as danger until his mother appeared against the sky waving something frantically to ward off the peril. And then the danger had made a vast, rumbling sound that had shaken Pacer as with physical force and had struck terror into him. And then it was over, and Ma was holding him, rocking him in her arms.

In later years, he'd told of this and both Pa and Ma had taken it for a vague recollection of the time Clint had shot the bear. Pacer was not sure. There was no bear in his memory or his dream. It was just an unthinking, deadly and formless danger.

Through the growing years he had recognized with a sharper pain than anyone else, he believed, how his mother stood in danger of being hurt in a thousand ways everytime anyone of any color came to their home. He'd

45

sensed the small changes in facial expressions, in tones of voices, when Ma came to the door, usually with an invitation to eat or rest. He'd sensed them because they were directed at him, too.

The first really bad time he'd had was when he was fresh-turned sixteen. Of a hot summer's day, a cavalryman and a half-breed Cherokee scout had walked their horses up to the house. Pacer had never seen soldiers before, and he'd rarely seen them since. These men had told Sam that they were out of Fort Davis, lost from the rest of their platoon, and they wanted to know how to get to The Crossing.

Ma had invited them to stay for dinner.

At first Pacer had felt almost a kinship for the scout. But he soon noticed that the scout was even worse than the white in his veiled disrespect for Ma. They were not so stupid as to allow Sam to notice, but they had ignored Pacer, thinking him too young to count.

Clint was out on the range, and Sam had stepped out to the corral briefly. Pacer had gone into the bedroom to get the good plates Ma kept in the chest there for special occasions.

He got back to the door in time to see the breed walk up behind his mother at the cooking board, put his arm around her and whisper something into her ear. At that point, he'd dropped the plates crashing to the floor.

The three people in the room whirled at the noise, the breed angered, the white soldier with a wide smile frozen on his face. Ma had been shocked and horrified, but as Sam came into the house she'd taken the broken dishes as the excuse for her upset.

"Oh, what a pity!" She moved away from the breed and knelt as though to put the shards back together.

"It's all right," Sam said soothingly. "We'll get some others."

Ten minutes after the soldier and the scout had left, Pacer made an excuse about wanting to check a wolf trap and rode away from the ranch. He'd circled wide, and when the two soldiers rode through Dead Man's Canyon, he'd been waiting in ambush for them.

His carbine was cocked and loaded and pointing steadily at them from twenty feet ahead and above. "Stop. Get off your horses."

The breed had looked up in startled surprise that changed to relief. "It's on'y the kid. Whatcha gonna do? Rob us?"

"I may kill you."

There was a tone in his voice that made the words true, and the breed considered a moment before speaking. "What's eatin' at you?"

"Off your horses. Now."

They'd got off grudgingly, and he'd disarmed them, then slapped their horses on down the canyon, weapons tied to the saddles.

"Whaddya go an' do that for?" the white soldier whined.

"Turn around."

When the white soldier's back was turned, Pacer swung the barrel of his carbine hard and fast, bringing it down with a hollow thunk on the man's head. The man had dropped senseless to the ground.

The breed was frightened now. "You can git y'self into trouble with the Army, kid," he said, staring into the muzzle of Pacer's carbine. "You better leave us be!"

Pacer was almost as tall as the breed, but not nearly so broad, so that when the boy walked back to his horse now and pushed the carbine into the saddle holster, the breed grinned. "Gonna fight me fair, huh?"

Wordless, Pacer moved toward him, his fists balled tight. The breed had tried to bull in through his defenses, and twice he succeeded, pounding through Pacer's flying fists, taking punishment but coming on. Each time, Pacer had stepped aside or back before the husky arms could wrap around him, and blood from a dozen cuts welled on the other's face.

The scout fell back, panting heavily, and reached for a large stone near his feet. He came at Pacer with the rock arching in a wide swing. The boy's knife flicked out as quick as the thinking of it, and as he ducked he chopped viciously at the upper arm and blood spurted out, darkening the cloth and pouring onto the ground.

Nearly helpless now, the man had stood on his feet while Pacer methodically and mercilessly beat his face almost beyond recognition. At last the breed fell, but he was not unconscious.

"I'm bleedin' t' death," he muttered through cut, swollen lips.

The boy looked down at the man and then, wordless, walked back to his horse and swung up. As he rode past the two men, the white soldier was moving groggily. Without glancing back, Pacer pushed his pony into a lope toward home.

He'd ridden up to the corral to find Clint back, helping Pa to shape a new branding iron over the blow-box fire.

Clint said, "What happened to you?"

"Horse almost stepped on a jackrabbit. Tossed me."

"How many times?"

"Just once. But good."

Sam looked up from the glowing rod of steel he was shaping. "You took a long way back from the wolf trap."

"Circled some."

And that was the end of that.

Except for one last thing Clint said that night when they were lying in their bunks. "You sure as hell landed hard on your knuckles." And then his older brother went to sleep.

There had been a time when Pacer was in love with Roslyn Pierce. That was when the Pierces had first come out here and had changed a barn—built years earlier by a settler who believed a barn more important than a house, then later deserted and, oddly, not burned by Comanche or Kiowa raiders—into a trading post. Now it was a general store, and The Crossing had sprung up around it. Roslyn had been a slender reed of a little girl, and the half-dozen times a year they had seen each other, she had been outgoing and warm toward both Pacer and Clint. Pacer had seen two changes in the girl since then. First, she'd gradually come to idolize Clint. Second, a wall, not of her own building, Pacer hoped, had come between her and him. He had been hurt at first, hurt deeper than even he let himself realize. Then the hurt had hardened into a

48

tough, realistic philosophy of living. He would keep a tight rein on the affection he had for anyone outside his family. "Don't play with fire, won't be burned," was what they said out here. And Pacer saw the sense of it. So he didn't love Roslyn any more—he told himself.

With the horses eagerly munching the corn behind him, Pacer started toward the house, where Ma was fixing dinner. It was, perhaps, the twenty-thousandth meal Ma had made in that house.

It would be the last.

CHAPTER EIGHT

Ma came to the porch to call Pacer when he was already
within talking distance of the house, and he saw her gaze
swing away behind him. Pacer turned and saw the Kiowas,
six of them, moving with no attempt to stay hidden. They
were half a mile off, coming on at a single-file lope.

"In the house, Ma."

Shutting and bolting the door behind him, Pacer levered
a fresh shell into his carbine, then closed the battle shutter
on the one open window. He was ready and waiting when
Buffalo Horn rode to the front of the house with his
warriors strung out beside him now.

Pacer had never seen a more impressive Indian. Big for
a Kiowa, almost as tall as a Cheyenne, he yet had the
square, muscular shoulders and thick, powerful chest of his
own tribe. His body was daubed with black spots, and
there were slender lines of black, white and yellow painted
horizontally across his broad face. He wore a buffalo-horn
warbonnet, from under which one wide, piercing eye
stared out with blazing intensity. Where the other eye had
been was a hollow, and the lid had widened and stretched
back in to line the emptiness.

Two of the five warriors with Buffalo Horn were braves
whom Pacer knew well. Two Moons was sitting his sleek,
handsome silver-dust stud next to Buffalo Horn. Two
Moons was about the same age as Pacer, and the two had
played Deer-to-the-River and Track-the-Animal when
Pacer, as a youngster, had gone with Ma to visit the
Kiowas. And later he and Two Moons had gone for short
hunts together and had shot Two Moons' target arrows.
Two Moons always won at archery, which pleased him always to laughter.

But the brave was not carrying target arrows now. They were war arrows, made with a barbed, slightly loose tip that would come off inside a wounded enemy when anyone tried to remove the shaft of the arrow.

At the far end of the six riders was Singing Hawk. Singing Hawk was silent to a point where strangers often wondered if he were deaf and dumb. Pacer had heard him say perhaps two words in the years that he had been visiting the Kiowas. Yet it was Singing Hawk whom Pacer liked and trusted most among the warriors he knew.

Now Buffalo Horn raised his right arm with the scalp-heavy lance in his hand. "The light of the sun is above us!" In his peculiarly harsh voice he added, "Now we will talk. Do you stay behind walls to talk to your Kiowa brothers?"

Pacer smiled tightly and without humor as he made his one-word answer: "Yes."

"Why is this?" the war chief demanded. "I come in the sun!"

"You come in the sun with many warriors. The walls are my warriors. We are alike."

Two Moons leaned forward over his stud's neck. "You are afraid because of what happened to the people in the valley of the winding river. You are a friend. It will not happen to you."

Pacer believed him. He was certain that these men had no intention of repeating the Howard massacre here and now. "I am not afraid, Two Moons. I am cautious."

"A rabbit is cautious," one of the strange warriors said, laughing.

Two Moons swung to stare angrily at him. "So is a wise mountain lion!"

Buffalo Horn turned to the men ranged alongside him and spoke in a low, fast voice. As he finished talking, the five of them wheeled their ponies and rode far up the flat, following the bank of the Little Mississippi.

When they at last pulled up to wait, their chief called to Pacer, "I will not talk through walls. I want to look in the face of a man I talk to."

Pacer's first thought was of the rear of the house. That wall had been built as a solid line of defense, but there

51

were four dry-packed clay loopholes in it. He crossed the room and silently cut through one of them with his knife. There was no one behind the wall. He would have gone out to speak with Buffalo Horn then, but still he hesitated because he was his mother's only defense.

"Go out," she told him, taking down the Collier's over-and-under that was pegged on the wall beneath the Sharps.

Pacer rarely wore a revolver, preferring to depend on the carbine he carried always. But now he went to his bunk and took out the well-oiled Joslyn side-hammer that Clint had given him five Christmases before. He loaded it and stuck it in his belt then took the Sharps and leaned it against the wall. It was, as always, loaded. He leaned the carbine next to it, and both long guns were in easy reach from where Ma stood watching out a loop-hole, the Collier's held ready in her hands.

"If I go down, shoot the bolt before you bother shooting at anything with a gun," he told her.

Pulling back the bolt, he opened the door and closed it tight behind him.

Buffalo Horn did a remarkable thing as Pacer walked out to stand a few steps from him. He swung down from his horse and moved so that he stood slightly before and to the side of the animal. That he should do this was a great compliment and a show of friendship, Pacer knew. A good war horse—and Buffalo Horn's deep-chested mare was a splendid animal—was a Kiowa's most prized and useful fighting possession, both offensively and defensively. Seated on the black mare, Buffalo Horn would have had a tremendous advantage of speed and power over Pacer. At the flick of a moccasin heel, the beast would have charged right on top of Pacer before he could have begun to get his Joslyn out of his belt. On foot, Buffalo Horn's strength as a warrior was more than cut in half, though he was still formidable.

"You came out of the house. I am glad." It was the closest a Kiowa could come to saying thank you.

Pacer nodded without speaking. He did not like leaving Ma inside the house alone, and he was impatient. This

52

sounded like the beginning of a long speech, so he made the throw-away sign, holding both hands closed before him, then sweeping them down away from him, snapping his fingers and opening the palms wide. This had many meanings, but now it meant "Throw away words that are not needed."

Buffalo Horn nodded once. "I am looking for warriors. I want many warriors. Many warriors are coming to my camp from the north. Many, many, many. The Kiowas have never been joined together. When the raiding moon comes, those who are together raid together. That is all. But there is no oneness. Under me, the nation can come together as one, and it will have great, great force. So much force that the Comanches, Shawnees, Cherokees, Apaches might want to ride with us. In this way, we might beat the whites in a grand battle. It is the only way. We cannot move to the setting sun. The whites are thick to the setting sun, along the Big Water. As thick as they are toward the rising sun. We have no place to go. We must fight with wisdom, or we will all be dead."

Pacer had, since his early days in the Kiowa camps, heard the theory of a unified Kiowa nation and the great strength it would have. But it had never been more than talk. The Kiowas had a loose, unorganized system of government—really no government at all. If a warrior had an idea for a profitable or exciting raid, he tried to convince some of the men in his tribe—which might consist of ten to forty people—that they should come with him. And that made him a chief on a purely temporary basis. No man had been strong enough to rise up as a substantial leader. Now, looking at the powerful, flashing-eyed man before him, Pacer realized Buffalo Horn might well be that leader.

"The raid in the valley of the winding river was nothing." Buffalo Horn shrugged scornfully. "Soon we will have the power to take whole white villages." He paused, letting those words sink into Pacer's mind. "You say you are not an enemy. You must be a friend. Will you ride with us?"

Pacer had seen this question coming. "With many warriors, one more warrior is not important."

"You are important. When the words go into the camps that a half-white has put himself on my side, it will help my medicine. My magic will be called stronger if you leave the safety and numbers of whites to ride free and vengefully with me." The chief paused once more. "And your family, this place here, will be safe if you ride with me."

"If I say no?"

"Then you are an enemy. You cannot stand on a line without moving."

"If I still say no?"

"This place here will be the first to go, when my strength is gathered from the north." Buffalo Horn's one eye glared with deep fire. "I will not have a half-Kiowa standing against me. It would lower my magic, if it came to be known."

Pacer did not agree with this, but arguing with the chief would be like arguing against a tree trunk. No answer came to him, and in the moment of waiting Ma's voice came from the house "Pacer, come in here a minute."

"I will return soon." Pacer walked back into the house and shut the door behind him.

Ma said, "I heard what he said."

Ma was more worried than Pacer had ever seen her before. Her eyes were wide, and she let go the Collier's with one hand and rubbed its palm on the apron over her long skirts. "I want to go see them," she said.

The words came on him so suddenly that Pacer's mind had to struggle to frame an answer. "The Kiowas?"

"Yes. I want to talk to Poh'sha-knay and to Lame Crow."

"But what for, Ma? This is no time to go traipsing around the country for any reason!"

"Lame Crow is a strong chief. Maybe he can stop all this—all this warring—before it starts."

"Ma, you couldn't be more wrong!" Pacer felt a desperation rising in him, for his mother had a look about her that he knew well—a look of absolute determination. She looked that way rarely, but when she did none of the

54

three men in her home could stand against her.

"Ma, you can't do one whit of good! No Kiowa cares what a woman says! The only reason Lame Crow ever talked to you was out of curiosity. And if you could by some miracle make him see your way, his opinion would mean nothing."

"I've got to try. I can't see our neighbors killed without trying. And other people we don't even know. I've got to try."

"I'm sorry, Ma. I can't let you go."

"I'm going. Would you hold me by force?"

"If need be."

She looked at him with a firm, set expression for several seconds. Then her gaze softened, and she said, "No, you couldn't lay a hand on me in strength."

He knew she was right.

"At least, Ma, don't act on it for a while," he said miserably. "Think on it. Talk to Pa and Clint first."

She shook her head. "No. They'd try to talk me away from it." She leaned the Collier's against the wall and stepped forward to touch Pacer's arm with her finger tips, but the pain and indecision did not leave his eyes.

"This is a thing I must do. No need for worry. They are my people."

Pacer said slowly, "If something happened to you I'd—"

"Nothing will. You'll be with me."

Pacer couldn't go against her any more. He had no choice but to give up. He turned and went back out to Buffalo Horn and said, "This is not a thing to be decided like this." He snapped his fingers. "There must be much thought. My mother would speak with her family. We will ride to your camp. And I will speak more to you of this. A fire and a pipe will give rightness to our words."

The chief turned and vaulted onto his black mare. Pacer thought that the one-eyed man was pleased, that he had hoped for any answer but a complete rejection, yet had not expected it.

"That is all good," Buffalo Horn said, swinging his horse around sharply on its braided buckskin single rein.

"It is all good. We will wait for you." He touched the mare lightly with his heels and the big black swung into a lope toward where the warriors were waiting up the Little Mississippi.

Pacer went to the corral to saddle horses for the ride, choosing a well-mannered dun mare for his mother. He put the rarely used sidesaddle on the dun's back and pulled a tight, hard hitch in the girth. If only he could go back into the house and think up some magic words to tell Ma so she would change her mind. Dropping the saddle flap back down over the cinch strap, he realized he was headed into a much more ticklish problem than this ride, than this visit to a Kiowa camp during the raiding moon. When the chips were down, the idea of his riding alongside Buffalo Horn in battle was downright laughable. Yet telling the chief this in the middle of his own village would be suicidal stupidity. Pacer would not be able to accept or reject Buffalo Horn's offer. It would take some tricky talking, for the one-eyed chief would be a hard man to fool or to lie to, and if he sensed the real purpose of Ma's visit . . .

Pacer led the horses to the house and let them stand, ground-reined. Inside, he said, "Ma, just one last time. As a special thing for me, will you forget this?"

She had put on her high-laced shoes, a wool shawl and a bonnet. Looking sadly at Pacer, she said, "No. I've got to try."

It was the first time within his remembrance that she had said no to him when he wanted a special thing. When, later, they rode to where the Kiowas were waiting for them, Pacer could not put down the feeling of tight, gray foreboding in his chest.

In his worry about known things, he had completely forgotten what he had seen earlier in the day: the tiny, faraway speck that had seemed to be a man running senselessly and waving his arms. He had forgotten that half vision, yet that was where the true danger lay.

CHAPTER NINE

Neither Sam nor Clint spoke as they rode in that night. From a mile or better away they first saw that the house was completely dark, and by common accord each broke his tired horse into a dead run. Their animals' heads were sagging with exhaustion as the two men slammed them into jarring halts before the front porch and rushed into the house.

In the still, dark house, Sam scratched a match to life and, in its flickering light, said, "No fight." He held the flame to the candle on the table.

Clint put the Colt, which he'd drawn toward the end of their ride, back into its holster. "Note," he said, glancing at the table.

Sam picked up the folded piece of paper. It was written in ink, in Pacer's large, studiedly careful handwriting. They read it together by the candlelight:

DEAR PA AND CLINT,
Ma took a notion to go see her sister, etc. . . . I told her no, but you know how she can be. So we're going. If it's no further than I think we will be back around midnight. I wish I could talk her into waiting, but you know Ma.
Resp. yrs.
PACER

Sam creased the paper slowly and put it back on the table. His forehead was wrinkled, his eyes staring intently at nothing. "No time for her to be doin' that."

"No." Clint took a long breath and said, "I'll change horses for us. And we can take off after them."

"Take off to where?"

"Well, Pa, it's got to be somewheres west of Buckskin Pass."

Sam glanced at the heavy, highly polished mantel clock above the fireplace. "About ten o'clock. Only a couple of hours till midnight. And there's a lot of land west of the pass. We'll give 'em those two hours. Then we'll go after them."

Clint knew that his father was right. Yet the thought of waiting two long hours didn't sit well with the tension building in his chest. "Maybe I could go. And you stay."

"No." Sam sat at the table, staring stonily ahead, one big hand resting in front of him. "We're already split two ways. We'll stick together."

To give himself something to do beyond caring for the horses they'd galloped in on, Clint saddled two fresh mounts and brought them to the front porch ready to ride. This done, he went into the bedroom and got Sam's double-barreled, ten-gauge shotgun. When he'd tied it to the saddle, he joined Pa at the table. "Depending on what happens," he said, "that scattergun might come in handy."

His father nodded.

They were both thinking that the Kiowas had a deathly fear of big-bore shotguns close up, and that the two of them might have to do their level best to break up an entire village before the night was done.

When Pacer, riding behind his mother in the single-file column, first saw the faces of the women in the Kiowa village, he knew with absolute finality that his mother was wasting her time. Nothing much could be told from the faces of the men. It was a point of manly living with them to maintain a certain stoicism before strangers, to guard their feelings behind tight, expressionless lips and eyes. A man riding in would not know whether a Kiowa warrior intended to give him a gift or cut his throat. But the women were the true gauge of the emotions in a village.

This was an arrogant, hostile camp, pleased with itself and confident of its powerful—perhaps numbering one hundred—gathering of warriors. They formed the hard core of renegade Kiowas in the south. Up north, the soldiers from Fort Sill—helped by particularly bad winters in the recent past—had subdued the other Kiowa villages. Sitting Bear and his sub-chiefs, White Bear and Big Tree, had been captured and killed, their people scattered, their power broken by the Yellow-stripes. Buffalo Horn was of a different mettle. He would not walk into white-soldier traps so easily. He was wily and foresighted.

The women in the village were not sullen and silent, as was usual. They looked at Ma and laughed scornfully at the way she was dressed, or spat, not exactly at her since she was with Buffalo Horn, but in her general direction.

Two Moons walked his horse abreast of Pacer now, and Pacer said, "My mother and I have few friends here."

The warrior shrugged. "Where I am you have a friend."

Pacer believed him. But as they rode through the lines of teepees, the yapping dogs and the openly derisive women, he suspected that Two Moons, with the possible excepting of Singing Hawk, was their only friend.

Ma's sister came to meet her when they approached the center of the camp. The years had laid waste to her, and though she was only two years older than Ma, she was already an ancient hag, toothless and wrinkled. The two of them went into Lame Crow's tent to talk, and Pacer rode on with Buffalo Horn, Two Moons and a gathering number of braves afoot.

It was late evening when a large fire was lighted in front of Buffalo Horn's teepee in the center of the camp. A deer was thrown on the fire. It had not been skinned or beheaded. This, Pacer knew, was to impress him with the wealth and strength of the camp. It was supposed to show that these people did not need the deerhide for buckskin, nor were they interested in the buck's horns for weapons. In theory, they had so much that they couldn't be bothered with such details. And Pacer felt a moment's sorrow for them that this pathetic gesture should be meaningful in their eyes.

Buffalo Horn gave Pacer the spot of ground to his right, which was a place of honor, and two of the chief's women cut chunks of half-burned, half-raw venison for them.

59

While the circle of braves ate, a warrior named Broken Hand told the joke about the two hunters. The story was based on an old custom that when two Kiowas hunted together it was considered polite for the one who shot game to give it to the other. And, therefore, since each of these men wanted a deer they came across, they put off shooting it, hoping the other would. So while they waited, each with an arrow loose in his bow, the deer escaped.

This was an old joke, but it always brought a roar of laughter.

As the men relaxed, the meat and warm fire gradually putting them in a contented, good-natured humor, Pacer could not find it in him to hate them. Fear them, if need be, yes. But not hate. Not just now, as they boasted and swapped stories among themselves like boys, content with what little they had.

Yet how different it had been at the Howards' a few nights ago!

When, later, the pipe was brought, Buffalo Horn lighted it with a live coal, which he held between two sticks. He blew four puffs, one in each direction, to invoke the good will of the gods in the east, west, south and north. Then he passed the long, slender pipe to Pacer, who puffed and in turn gave it to Two Moons on his right.

As each man puffed from the pipe, Pacer steeled himself for the talk that was about to begin. How to refuse Buffalo Horn without seeming to refuse? Ask for more time to think about it? That seemed best. Or, if things got too tight, do the best job of lying he could and tell the Kiowas he would ride with them. Anything, just so Ma got out of here all right.

To Pacer's complete surprise, Buffalo Horn did not bring the subject up. The chief talked of the numbers of warriors he expected to join him from the north. He spoke of the last six winters—"three and three more"—and said that since they had all been light winters, the seventh would probably be brutally cold and long.

The other warriors told stories of battles and hunts and asked Pacer occasional questions about white people and the way they lived. "Is it true," Broken Hand wanted to know, "that the earth is round and that white men live on all sides of it?"

Pacer nodded. "Yes, that is true."

"Then why don't the men on the bottom fall off?" Broken Hand's shrewd eyes were filled with laughter and Pacer knew it would be useless to continue.

An old man named Smoking Treetop said, "I saw a drawing in a white man's book once of a great mountain lion on which someone had painted lines. Why would they paint lines on a mountain lion?"

After some time, Pacer realized that Smoking Treetop had seen a picture of a tiger and attempted to explain a little about the big cat, using ringtails and coatis as examples.

When the warriors began to drift away to their tents to sleep, Buffalo Horn stood up. Pacer got to his feet also and, realizing instinctively that it was something he must say, said, "We did not talk about this thing I came to talk about."

The chief looked at him, his one eye glinting in the low flames of the dying fire. "My spirit reached out and touched you, and I knew it would not be good to speak of it. You are not ready. If I had asked you, you would have said no, or you would have not told the truth, and I would have known it. And since I knew it, the others would have known. Either way I would have had to kill you."

"It was good that you came to see and talk to these men. You are closer to us now than you were before. That is the only way you can be made to join us. For while I can kill you, I know I cannot bend you through fear." The chief hesitated. "Think of this. The gods will be with us in this stand against the whites. Have we gone out to take their land? No. It is they who come against us, forever cutting deeper into our land, forever taking, forever pushing.

"Our fight is a just one. We will talk again." Buffalo Horn turned and walked toward his teepee.

Two Moons approached Pacer and said, "If you are ready to ride back, I will go with you a distance."

They got their horses and led them to Lame Crow's

tent, and Pacer leaned down and stepped through the leather flap. His mother was sitting on a round, woven rug with her sister Poh'sha-knay and Lame Crow. None of them was speaking, and Pacer could see that his mother had long since given up talking to them.

"Ready, Ma?"

She nodded and stood up. From somewhere about her long, heavy skirts she produced a bag of sugar and gave it to Poh'sha-knay. It was stuff she knew her sister loved and rarely had. Then, without speaking, she stepped out of the tent and Pacer followed her.

The three of them rode silently from the camp that now, aside from an occasional dog's grumbling and low snores from some of the teepees, was as quiet as death. Pacer noticed that there were look-outs stationed beyond the camp. They passed one in the moonlight who raised his hand in recognition of Two Moons. That a Kiowa chief could do such a remarkable thing—convince his men of the wisdom of maintaining a night watch—was proof in itself that he was an outstanding leader. In every way, Pacer decided, Buffalo Horn was a man to be reckoned with.

When they were beyond hearing of the village, Ma leaned her head forward, her right elbow resting on her right knee, which was crooked around the sidesaddle horn. She began to weep.

Pacer swung his horse closer to the dun she was riding and reached out to put his arm gently on her back. "Ma . . ." There was nothing more he could say.

"They wouldn't even listen to me," she murmured. "Neither of them. They said I wasn't a Kiowa any more, nor a white either. My own sister said I was nothing!"

Pacer put a firmer pressure against her back. "You did the best could be done, Ma."

Understanding their words, Two Moons rode slightly ahead, embarrassed and not quite sure what else to do. They rode without speaking for nearly two hours.

It was a little beyond midnight, and they were not far from the western entrance to Buckskin Pass when Two Moons decided to break the silence.

62

"It is a long time, it seems in my mind, since we have ridden together."

Pacer nodded. "Yes."

Now Two Moons plunged into the news he had been holding back through most of the ride. "As a friend, you might want to know. I am going to take a woman."

Pacer glanced at his mother in the moonlight. She had stopped her weeping. Her face was set in lines of deep concern, and she stared straight ahead, oblivious to what he and Two Moons were saying.

Two Moons had dropped back so that the three of them were riding abreast, with Pacer in the center, as they came closer to the dark shadows of Buckskin Pass.

Pacer said, "It is a good thing. Do I know the woman?"

"No. She is very strong. A good woman, and young." Two Moons put one hand on the neck of his handsome silver-dust stud. "Her father would give her to me for this horse, but I refused. Instead, I will give him three other horses." He thought about it a moment before saying, "Truly, I would not give this one horse for three women."

Suddenly, with complete unexpectedness, the wild man appeared from behind the large rock in the moonlight ahead of them. The thought of the tiny, faraway speck of movement he'd seen earlier that day came rushing back to Pacer's mind as the man shrieked, "Kill you! Kill you!" and began shooting with an odd-appearing object in his hand that at first did not look like a gun but was.

Will Howard had been crazed and dying for more than four days. With the almost impossible tenacity of the insane, he had wandered nearly fifty erratic, stumbling miles toward the west, eating nothing, drinking rarely at the lonely streams he came upon.

There were only two things that Howard was aware of. One was to kill Kiowas, or any other Indians. The second was that sickening night, the night when the Kiowas had come. Beyond that, he remembered nothing.

His memory began with the moment he and his brother

63

walked from the house in the early evening. Why they had gone out, he did not know.

"You got the withal t' roll a smoke?" his brother Tom had asked him.

And those words, stored in the dim recesses of his mind, were the last words Will was ever to hear.

There was a savagely soft whump of sound and Tom arched back suddenly as though to yawn. As he twisted Will saw the arrow buried deep in his back.

The Kiowas were on them before Tom fell to the ground. Will reached for his brother to stop his fall, and a savage was suddenly there, slamming at Tom's head with a war ax.

Will had a brief, flooding sensation of shame that he had not stopped that crushing war ax before he realized that he was in trouble himself.

It was not until much later that he knew he had been hit with an arrow, too. And a warrior's left hand was clutching his jacket from behind, leaving the brave's right hand free to swing a tomahawk at the back of Will's head. It was that clutching hand that slowed Will down from helping Tom, and it was the fact that he tried to help Tom that saved his own life. The swinging tomahawk missed a square cut as Will lurched forward. It simply sliced away a little of the flesh on the right side of his skull.

Will whirled, trying to grapple with the savage behind him. And that was when his father made the fatal mistake of trying to save his sons' lives. Old Man Howard slammed the door open and stood there firing with a rifle into the now yammering, charging mass of Kiowas. The first slug hit the warrior holding Will's jacket, and Will stumbled toward the doorway of the house. Bullets and arrows were pounding into the doorframe and into the front of the house, and as Will got within reaching distance of his father, a long, gaily colored shaft appeared in Old Man Howard's throat. It was as though the arrow had not been shot into his throat, but rather as if it was simply, suddenly there.

Will's right foot was, vaguely, a bother to him now, and, ignoring it as best he could, he pushed his father back into the house and turned to bolt the door.

It was too late.

His mother and sister, Dorothy, were standing with their backs to the fireplace, his mother whitefaced, his sister equally terrified but firing with a revolver at the savages whooping only a step behind Will.

Three Kiowas crashed into the slamming door and burst into the room.

Will, nearly blinded by his own blood by now, leaped halfway across the room so that he landed flush on his chest on the kerosene lamp burning there. His chest was burned and punctured by splinters of glass, but the room was in darkness.

From then on, there was no accurate memory. Will knew he had killed at least one of the first three Kiowas to come in. He didn't know what had happened to his mother.

When the dark room was swarming with Indians, he had opened the trap door that Old Man Howard had put in eight years before. It was a miracle that he had maybe three seconds by himself in the dark corner of the room where the trap door was, and he let himself down into the small escape tunnel that led about forty feet from the house to where tall grass had been purposely let grow. Somehow he had thought Dorothy was with him as he crawled the length of the tunnel and got his head against the three short planks forming a sod-covered trap door in the tall grass. He shoved one of the planks aside and pushed his head up above ground. Then he could move no more. His back seemed to be clamped in a giant vise and his foot throbbed unmercifully. He thought he was going to die, though his eyes were open and he could see with uncommon clarity the darkened house and the savages swarming into and around it.

They dragged Dorothy out of the house, and it was in the next few minutes that Will Howard went insane.

Unable to move, he could see—and he could hear her screaming, screaming, screaming.

Much later, the Kiowas had thrown what was left of Dorothy back into the house. They tossed Tom's body in

65

after her and fired the house. Then they had ridden away whooping into the night.

Will had dragged himself up onto the ground, and while it was still night he'd gotten some small strength back—enough to follow the Kiowas with deadly, lunatic desperation. He knew he was limping. But he did not know, ever fully, that half of his left heel had been blown off by a piece of lead the size of a hawk's egg, fired from an ancient musket.

He had stumbled perhaps two miles before he realized that somehow he had picked up and shoved into his belt the Howards' old four-barrel Lancaster. A cumbersome hand gun, it nevertheless packed a fearful wallop, each of the four barrels holding a big .455 slug. This, he realized dully, would be better for killing Kiowas than his bare hands.

On his second night of wandering, he had stretched out on the ground briefly and turned onto his back. That was when he knew there was an arrow there for the shaft broke under his weight and an almost paralyzing pain shot through his back.

It was night—how many nights later, Will did not know—when he reached the far end of Buckskin Pass. He knew he had been falling often now, and, though time meant nothing to him, it had once taken him more than an hour to get back on his feet.

And then he had seen the three riders coming toward him. One Kiowa. And, Will knew with the cunning of insanity, two Kiowas dressed as whites, pretending not to be what they were.

As the sound of the first shot filled the still night air, Pacer's reaction was the quickest, but it was Two Moons—quickly kneeing his splendid silver-dust stud forward—who came closest to averting tragedy.

Pacer swung his animal instantly to the right, covering his mother's body with his own. Two Moons charged straight at the filthy, blood-caked figure in the shadows.

Will Howard's first shot went wild. He pulled back on the single trigger that fired at four points during the long pull, sending the second .455 slug into Two Moons' face, and the warrior died soundlessly, thrown backward off his horse. The silver-dust, smelling the blood, swung to the side, shying away from Howard.

Pacer's Joslyn side-hammer was in his hand now. His mother's dun reared in fright and plunged a step ahead as Pacer tried to get off a shot at the crazed man still facing them. The percussion cap was a dud and did not go off as the hammer fell. At that moment Howard got off his third shot.

Ma said, "Oh!" as though something had disturbed her slightly, and Pacer knew she had been hit. In desperation, not knowing what was wrong with his Joslyn, he charged at full gallop toward the man, hoping at least to draw fire away from his mother.

Howard's last shot was pulled off as Pacer swooped down upon him, leaning far out of the saddle to use his revolver as a club. The fourth shell missed Pacer, but his jacket was blackened with powder burn. His gun barrel slammed against Howard's head and the man went down. And as he struck, Pacer threw himself from the saddle.

As Howard struggled to his feet, Pacer was on him, slashing furiously back and forth with the steel barrel, his left hand clutching Will Howard's torn shirt front to keep him upright. Pacer used his gun until his arm grew numb, then released his hold and stepped back. The man's head sank onto his chest and he sagged forward, sprawling on the wet grass. He no longer felt the shooting pain of the arrowhead and broken shaft he still carried in his back.

Only now did Pacer realize that his assailant had been Will Howard. But the dead man's face, half turned into the pale moonlight, meant nothing beyond passing recognition. Belting his gun, he turned quickly and ran to his mother's side.

She was clinging weakly to the skittery dun, and as Pacer got to her she slipped out and away from the saddle. He caught her as she fell, lowering her gently to the ground.

Without actually dwelling on it, Pacer had always thought that if his mother were ever seriously hurt, he would panic, become blindly helpless and lost. But as his hand came away from her slender waist, soaked with blood, and he heard her breathing become harsh and labored, an icy, intense calmness came over him. He probed with steady, deft fingers. The slug had entered his mother's left side under the rib cage and had gone out her back, a few inches from her spinal cord. He tore strips from her underskirts and fashioned rough bandages which he tied firmly into place with long, thin strips. He was wondering about the safest way to get her home when he heard the sound of horses coming fast.

Pacer ran to his horse, which was standing stiff-legged a few yards away. Whipping his carbine out of the saddle holster, he led the animal back toward his mother.

He placed the horse just so, ready to trip it up—shoot it if necessary—to form a breastwork to protect his mother. He leveled his carbine over the saddle toward the sound of the approaching horses. As the sound became clearer, he recognized the hoofbeats of only two horses.

He was standing in the best defensive position he knew how to arrange when Sam and Clint rode out of Buckskin Pass and into the moonlight of the flats.

CHAPTER TEN

Clint was the first to dismount, and he had the shotgun in his hands when his feet touched ground. He'd seen everything there was to see, and he said, "Any more to worry about?"

"No. Guess not." Pacer came from behind his mount and nodded at the corpse of Will Howard. "It was him. Alone."

Clint knelt beside his mother, then glanced quickly at Two Moons and Howard. "Nothing to be done for them?" It was a statement more than a question. "Let's get Ma home."

"Hand her up to me." Sam spoke in a low, calm voice that betrayed his fear and sorrow more than anything else could. "I'll carry her back."

The two sons lifted their hard-breathing mother up to their father, who seemed more than ever now to be a giant in the saddle, and he carried his wife's slight weight easily in his arms.

The three of them, Clint leading the dun, rode slowly back through the pass and across the wide, silver-toned prairie to their home. After they were in the house, with Ma placed comfortably in the bed, Sam checked her wounds and rebandaged them. He said just two words: "What happened?"

"Will Howard jumped up and let fly," Pacer answered tonelessly. "Hit her with one of his shots."

"You do all them things to Will?" Clint asked.

"No. He was already hurt—a long time before. Maybe in that raid. But I guess I killed him. Hitting him with the Joslyn."

"Poor fool must have been half loco," Clint said.

69

"Wasn't like Will to cut loose like that."

"You forgivin' him?" Pacer's voice moved from the toneless quality into a sound of angry disbelief.

Clint shook his head. "No. You hadn't killed him, me or Pa would have."

Sam straightened up from the bed. "All can be done by us. Need a doctor now."

"I'll go to The Crossing and get Phillips," Clint said.

The three men glanced at one another. Each of them understood, without anything being said, that there was the question of whether Dr. Phillips would come.

Clint glanced once at his mother lying still and weak in the bed. As he started from the room he said over his shoulder, "I'll fetch him, all right."

Outside, as Clint was mounting his horse, Pacer joined him. "Pa'll want to stay, but two might be better at fetching than one."

The two brothers rode at a hard long-legged lope toward The Crossing. But their start was so late that it was high morning before they got there.

At the nooning sun, they rode toward the buildings that formed the small town, and as they approached, several men darted back and forth on the single short street and then disappeared.

Two men walked into the middle of the street and stood waiting for the brothers. From still far out, Clint and Pacer recognized Dred Pierce and Ben Ford.

When the mounted men were within hailing distance, Dred Pierce held up one hand and shouted, "Don't come no closer!" He ignored Pacer, speaking only to the older brother in his high, angry voice.

"No Indian lover wanted here, Clint! You had your chance an' chose to pass it by!"

Clint pulled his horse to a stop and called, "We're coming in, Dred."

"Like hell!" Pierce waved one arm in a sweeping circle around him. "There's eight, ten men in the windahs and such around here, just itchin' for their chance t' shoot an Indian lover." He glanced at Pacer for the first time. "Or a Indian!"

70

"No need for fear about running off our cows, Dred," Clint called, now walking his mount toward the two men at a slow pace. "We need Doc Phillips. Ma's been hurt."

Clint and Pacer were almost into the town now, and Dred yelled, "You stay put!" From half a dozen windows and a couple of doors on the street, the brothers could see jutting rifle barrels, their muzzles slanting at angles toward where they sat their horses.

Clint's voice took on a hard edge. "Maybe you didn't hear me right, Dred."

"I heard. How's she hurt?" It was cold curiosity.

Pacer blurted out in sudden, furious impatience, "Will Howard shot her! And we ain't got time to sit around talking about it!"

Ben Ford hooked his thumbs through the shoulder straps of his leather blacksmith apron and frowned in slow thought. "Will Howard's still alive?"

There was a moment of hard silence, and then Clint said, "He was."

Angus Pierce was holding a rifle on them from a window in the second story of the Pierce store. He leaned partly out and demanded, "If he'd dead, who kilt 'im?"

"Me!" Pacer's hand went to the Joslyn. "And I'm about to up my score if—"

Clint's big left hand grabbed Pacer by the shoulder and pulled hard, almost dragging him out of the saddle, as Angus raised his rifle and fired. Even so, the shell whipped by close enough for Pacer to hear it.

"Hold up, Angus!" Dred bellowed, and Roslyn appeared beyond the window, hauling her bulky brother away more with her voice than her slight body.

"If shooting starts," Clint told the older Pierce, "I'll stay alive long enough to kill you."

"It won't, if'n you go now. But I'll see to it the Rangers in Austin get word about the killin' of Will Howard."

Ignoring Dred now, Clint turned in the saddle toward Dr. Phillips' house and shouted, "Phillips! I want to talk to you!"

After a few seconds the door opened slowly and the doctor came out onto the boardwalk before his home. He

71

was a small man of about forty, and his bearing matched his size. His usual nervousness and lack of certainty was stamped on him now even more plainly.

"What . . . what do you want, Clint?"

"You heard our talk out here."

"Well, yes. Parts of it."

"Then get your horse. You're coming with us."

Phillips glanced helplessly from Clint to Dred. Pierce said, "We don't take to that kind of talk here. Doc'll do what he wants to do. He don't have to be pushed into nothing."

Ben Ford nodded and grumbled deep in his throat, "Dred's right. It's a free country. 'Sides, I'd rather he didn't go, and I'll say why. With all that's goin' on around here, and what's like to come, The Crossin' may need a doctor sooner'n we think. Case of an all-out war, this is where the ranchers'll be comin' to. Some of 'em is goin' t' need doctorin'. An' The Crossin' itself might get hit. Things bein' what they are, it's a risk for a man to ride clear out to your place, Clint. Even if you was just ordinary ranchin' people."

"Phillips!" Clint said hard and sharp, "our ma is hurt bad! You coming to her, or you want to be carried?"

"I said no threats, goddammit!" Dred bellowed. "He'll do what he pleases!"

The doctor swung his gaze uncertainly from Dred to Clint. At last he said, "Clint, I got to do what these people want me to do. They're my people. You understand?"

Phillips had looked at death many times. But never had he looked at living death as it showed in the faces of the two young men sitting tall and furious in their saddles. Pacer's expression was as hard as iron, and only his eyes showed the sparks of deep-flaming rage within him. Clint's face was calmer, more thoughtful, but equally deadly. Phillips felt his knees shake suddenly. Instinctively, he bent his legs so that the shaking stopped, and he turned to Dred. "What does The Crossing want me to do, Dred?"

Pierce thought about the question a little. "I know how I feel. Can't say for the others. Like Ben says, this is a free country. I say let's take a vote. Most of 'em want you t' go—all right. They want you to stay, that's all right, too."

"I already said no," Ford told Phillips. "What you say, Dred?"

"I speak the same."

Ben Ford left Pierce and went to one side of the short street, asking through the windows and doors what each man's vote was.

Both brothers knew, before he'd covered one side of the short street, what the answer was going to be.

In a low voice Pacer said, "Cover me, Clint. I'll get him."

"No." The answer was an order, spoken low but strong. "We'll get him. But two dead men are no good. Take it easy."

Dred, hearing the steady string of "No's," said, "Clint, you're a disappointment to me. You could've been somethin'. You could've come with us. Why, Clint, you might've even married Roslyn. And you threw all this over—maybe ownin' my store here someday—just for your—your family."

"Dred," Clint told him flatly, "your girl is not worth a son of my mother and my father." He turned to Pacer. "The vote's gone against us already. Let's go."

They turned their horses and rode away from The Crossing.

When they were out of gunshot range, the muscles in Pacer's back relaxed, and he said, "You said we'd get him. How?"

"Don't know just yet. Thinking on it."

"We'll have to take him by force."

"Yeah." Clint turned to his brother. "You count too far on strength. Thinking is better."

When they had got to the top of a slanting rise beyond The Crossing, they turned back for one last look. The town was settling down. People were wandering about the single street, some of them watching to make sure the brothers had left, and behind one of the houses, two children had come out to play.

Clint said, "Those two kids. One of them is Phillips' little girl."

73

"Yeah." Pacer nodded and they rode on out of sight of those who were watching.

Once out of sight, they stopped and Pacer said, "Not a bad idea. I should do it. That kind of thing I got you whipped at."

"Umm." Clint's eyes went to a rock a quarter of a mile to their left. "I'll watch from there. Soon as you're on 'em, I'll come down fast."

Pacer dismounted and Clint took his horse to lead it to the rock. By the time Clint was behind the big boulder, the horses tied behind him and he himself invisible to the people below, Pacer was out of sight.

It took time. In tracking and remaining unseen, the essential is time. There was nearly a mile of unbroken country, of flat, monotonous plain, leading to The Crossing. And this was what Pacer had to travel unseen. He entered a gully that helped a little and followed it swiftly, at a left angle, bringing him closer to the house where the children were playing.

Next he was up on the flats, his stomach pressed hard against the sandy earth, crawling closer and closer to his goal. He took advantage of every inch of cover afforded him—a sagebrush, a natural mound of dirt, a saguaro cactus. His sharp eyes detected immediately if someone at The Crossing was watching or facing in his direction, and during those times he was as still and unmoving as a dark rock on the ground. It took him more than an hour to get within a hundred feet of the two children, who were still playing. Maggie, Dr. Phillips' six-year-old girl, went into the house. Pacer waited patiently, and after a time she came out again.

And then he was on his feet, running tall and swift toward the children. He was on them before they knew anyone was on the flat behind the house.

Pacer grabbed the little girl and lifted her into his arms. "Maggie," he said. "You know me."

The girl said, "Oh!" in startled surprise, and then she looked up into Pacer's face and said, "Sure. But did you have to scare me?"

He hugged her gently. "I'm playing a game with you,
74

Maggie. Didn't you know that?"

"Well, I didn't know it before, Pacer. But all right."

"We're going to get your pa in on the game. Would you like that?"

She shrugged with eloquent indifference. "He doesn't play too good."

Pacer yelled toward the house, "Phillips! Come on out here!"

The doctor came to the back door, as others in the town came from around the house to see what the shouting was about.

"Put her down!" Phillips shrieked. "Leave her alone!"

"Get your horse and get out here, and hurry!"

Maggie shifted uncomfortable in his arms. "You sound like you're mad."

"It's okay, Maggie. Part of the game."

"I don't like this game."

"Please. Please, little girl. Play it with me a little bit. It's important to me. Will you?" he whispered.

"Well, for a little while."

Pacer whipped out his Joslyn as Phillips and the others started toward him.

"You—you wouldn't hurt her!" the doctor shouted.

Pacer hugged the girl again gently to show her his own feelings and to reassure her. He called back, "Phillips! Get that horse and get out here fast!"

Phillips disappeared around the house at a dead run. Dred Pierce and Ben Ford were among those who had been brought by Pacer's shouts. As Pacer heard the pounding hoofs that would be Clint coming in with both horses, Dred yelled, "You hurt that child and you'll be dead in the minute!"

Putting his lips close to the girl's ear, Pacer laughed low and pleasantly. "Grownups never know how to play, do they?"

She shook her head. "This is . . . this is funny playin', Pacer. I don't like it! Put me down." And tears of fear and bewilderment came to her eyes.

"Please. Please don't cry," he said to her. "I'll put you down in a minute. You know I will."

Clint charged to a pounding halt near Pacer and the girl, and he was out of the saddle as the horses came to a stop. "Phillips is getting a horse."

"I know."

Clint pulled his Colt and aimed it at the people who were hesitantly advancing toward them. "Pierce, if any man moves closer, I'll shoot your head off."

Phillips appeared, mounted.

"Get your bag!" Clint commanded.

The doctor almost fell off the pinto in getting down and was back out of the house, the bag clutched in one hand, in a few seconds.

Clint said, "You others. Anybody follows up, there'll be pure hell to pay."

Phillips rode to where they were and Pacer put Maggie down.

Then, with the doctor between them, the two brothers rode fast toward Flaming Lance.

CHAPTER ELEVEN

They had gone less than two miles when they realized they were being followed. At an arroyo through which they had just passed, they waited a few precious minutes in ambush. They had seen but one rider, a speck at least a mile and a half away, and now they found that the rider was alone, not the leader of a group.

It was Roslyn Pierce.

As she burst at a full gallop through the narrow arroyo, Clint called, "Stop!" Holstering his gun, he rode out to her, and Pacer followed with Dr. Phillips within arm's reach.

The girl's eyes were wide with fright and excitement. "I came to help. If your ma's hurt enough for you to do what you did, then she'll need care beyond the doctor. She'll need nursing."

Neither Clint nor Pacer could frame an answer, for they understood what her coming meant. At last Clint said simply, "Let's go."

The four of them rode on to the west, pushing their ponies at the fastest pace possible.

Once they stopped long enough to let their mounts drink briefly from a small stream. Clint reined his horse in next to Roslyn's and said, "What you're doing—it's thought of highly."

She stared at him steadily. "No need."

"For me there is. You're doing a brave thing for Ma— a thing no one else was strong enough to do."

"I love your ma." Her voice was firm and low. "But I'm doing this for you, Clint."

He looked at her sharply, surprised. "Me? Why?"

"Because—because I want you. As my husband. And

you couldn't respect a person who didn't come with you in your time of need."

"I wish you hadn't put that thought in words, Ros. It doesn't make me think more of you. It just makes me think more."

Pacer was already moving across the small creek with Phillips close behind him. Clint swung out with Roslyn riding at his side, and the four moved on at the same fast pace.

Phillips did not try to escape. There were two reasons for this: First, he actually felt safer with these two bronzed, hard-eyed men than he would have felt alone on the barren, frightening immensity of these Western prairies. Secondly, he knew that if he were to try to get away from the two brothers, he would at best be recaptured with impatient ease—or at worst he would be killed.

They rode on at a steady pace and after early dark they arrived at the Flaming Lance ranch.

There was no one there.

That day was the longest Sam had ever known. Ma began to worsen in the afternoon, and chills set in. Try as he would to warm and comfort her, she shook violently from time to time, and her breathing in these spells was little more than desperate gasps for air.

Several times he tried to feed her some warm, thin soup, but she would not take any. Suffering the torture of a strong man who is helpless, Sam saw the sun move with maddening slowness into the west as the day grew to a close. His concern was now multiplied, for his boys should have been back by now. He was afraid to think of what might have happened at The Crossing.

Twice during his lonely vigil over his wife, Sam knew that she was conscious. Neither time did she speak, but her eyes opened and focused on him and she smiled. He believed that she did not have the strength to do more, for she had lost a lot of blood. He was afraid, too, that she might be bleeding internally, though he had stanched the flow from the ugly, jagged wounds in her side and back.

Each time her eyes cleared and focused on him, he

78

moved quickly to her and held the one hand showing above the Indian blankets. Each time he had a moment to murmur something encouraging and hopeful to her, and then she was gone, back to her own world of half-dreams.

He kept the fire going in the fireplace. He heated bricks, blanket-wrapped them, and laid them beside her to keep the little warmth she had in her body. In his last roundup ride with Clint, Sam had twisted his recently broken leg in the stirrup, and it was beginning to pain him. When he went out to get wood for the fire the morning after his sons had left for The Crossing, he realized he was limping, but he paid it no heed.

At full dusk, Ma seemed to rally. The chills were not upon her any more, and her labored breathing settled to long, easy intakes of air. It was then that Sam decided to spend a few, short minutes caring for the stock that had been untended all day. Before he left, he drew back the shutters on the bedroom window, in case Nettie called to him. Hurrying as fast as he could on his hurt leg, he fed the horses in the corral and barn, and milked the one milk cow. It took him only a quarter of an hour, and during this time his senses were acutely turned for danger, his eyes and ears constantly probing the dark that had settled over the prairie. Perhaps it was this attention to the unknown that caused him to miss the sight and the small sound of Ma leaving the house, for when he got back, she was gone.

He knew she had gone to the west or to the north, for the other two directions would have taken her close to the barn, where he would have seen her. Hatless, coatless, he limped swiftly from the house and moved out onto the still, moonless flats. In his mind, he was not an older man, nor his wife a mature woman with grown sons. He was simply himself, as he had always been, with no thought of youth or age, only the thought of weakness or power within him. She was the timid young girl he had married so long ago who had been terrified at the sight of a sparrow frightening a rabbit into flight, who had been willing to battle a bear with no more weapon than a water pail. It was these thoughts of her that caused him to call her by

79

the name he'd used when their world was young. "Nettie!" he cried out to the darkness surrounding him. "Where are you, Nettie?"

Ma's mind had been clearer than anyone knew. She was aware of most everything that had happened from the time she had been hurt, when Pacer had helped her out of the saddle. She'd wanted to stop him from tearing her skirts, but she was so weak she could not speak. And, in a pleasant, detached way, she had enjoyed the ride home in Sam's arms.

She knew she had slept a good deal, for her dreams had centered around a concept that was new and delightful to her. This big country that she knew and loved was made suddenly much bigger in her dreams. And the Pecos Mountains were bigger and farther away from Flaming Lance. And, westward, the land went on forever. There was room and room to spare for everyone who loved this big land. The Kiowas could hunt and raid among themselves and against other tribes as they had done for untold years, and the whites could raise their cattle and set up their towns, and neither would interfere with the other. It was that simple in her mind.

She knew that twice when she awoke Sam was there at her side, and she wished she had the strength to tell him how much she loved him, but all she could do was smile. She wondered where Pacer and Clint were. Probably out on the range, working cattle. So much, always so much to do.

The third time she awoke, Sam was not there. She turned her head to look about the room—at the log walls Sam had planed so carefully, the heavy chest he had fitted so meticulously, the wooden pegs he had driven into the chinks in a neat row across one wall. Sam. She began to smile. Her eyes reached the open window and her smile caught halfway. Through the rough-cut aperture she could see a square of dark sky, and almost directly in the center of it she saw something . . . something. Frowning, she whispered to herself, "The Black Star?"

There was suddenly a force within her that allowed her

to get up and out of bed, to do what she knew must be done. The Bible was on a shelf near the bed, but her eyes swept across it and beyond it without hesitation. She was going to die, and this was no time for books.

Walking softly, without realizing she was in her bare feet, she crossed the room and the kitchen and went out into the dark, cool night air.

Rounding the house, she started walking at an angle to the left of the North Star. The Kiowas had known for generations that those who die go to a place—without being defined too carefully and therefore destroyed —somewhere west of the North Star. That is where wait those gods who are, among all the supernatural beings, the most kindly and understanding. And it is in that general direction that spirits go to join those gods.

Moving northwest, occasionally tripping slightly on sagebrush branches and stones, she struggled toward this place.

After what seemed a very long time, she fell down and could not get back up. It was then that she heard Sam shouting, "Nettie! Nettie!"

He was still far away, and he should not come here with her, but she was somehow glad of it.

Then Sam came bounding across the plain in great, leaping strides that, despite his bad leg, made her think of the great runners she had known in her tribe, men who could race with horses and not be exhausted from the effort.

He almost passed her in the dark, would have passed her, except that his eyes were frantically searching the shadows on all sides. He saw her stretched on the ground and ran to kneel at her side.

"Oh, Nettie!" He was weeping, and his words came brokenly. "You shouldn't—shouldn't—"

But she wasn't listening to him. Puzzled, her forehead creased, she searched the skies for the Black Star. It had disappeared. Then, clutching her husband's strong arm held protectively across her, she said softly, "Sam, look! Do you see it?" Her eyes were fixed on a spot far across the plain, and they sparkled with a childlike wonder.

81

"Don't you see it? It's a candle! A lighted candle, and someone is carrying it toward us!"

She tried to raise herself on one elbow, but the exertion proved too much. As Sam quickly slid his arm under her, she fell back.

"Nettie! Nettie!"

How long he stayed kneeling beside her, clutching her to him, trying to force and call life back into her, Sam did not know.

When at last he picked her up to carry her home, he saw through tear-filmed eyes that the quarter-moon was swimming over Banner Pass to the northwest. And he wondered if that had been what Nettie had seen, or if she had truly seen, with an inner sight that only she had, a glowing, dancing point of distant light that had been a candle.

CHAPTER TWELVE

There were four horses in front of the house as Sam carried his wife in from the prairie. One of the four was standing with its head nearly between its front legs from exhaustion. Another had gone down on its side and was dying.

Clint had been at the corral, cutting fresh horses for the search they were going to make. Now he came pounding across the yard in a heavy, tired run that was no less swift for his tiredness.

"Pa?"

Pacer came out of the house, having heard Clint's running footsteps, and moved quickly toward the other two.

Sam said just one word: "Dead." Then he continued toward the house.

Clint murmured, "Oh, God! Ma . . ." and Pacer said nothing.

The three of them went into the kitchen of the house, where Dr. Phillips and Roslyn had just got up from the table. Sam continued on into the bedroom and placed the slender, light body tenderly on the bed.

Phillips came into where the other three men were standing silently, looking at the still figure. He reached for her pulse, and it was Clint who said, "Don't touch her."

There was a softness yet an intensity in the voice that caused Phillips' short hair on the back of his neck to rise. "Just wanted to make sure she was gone."

"You already made sure—" Clint's voice was still soft, still on the edge of murder—"when you wasted time at The Crossing."

Phillips went out of the room to where Roslyn had now

built up the fire and was preparing to cook a meal, moving about the kitchen silently and deliberately, knowing what she was doing was right, even though no one would eat.

They buried Ma late that night on a rise a short distance from the house. The three men worked by lamplight at the grave, and they made it deep and proper. They had already fashioned a coffin in the barn, and Roslyn had dressed Ma in her best clothes.

Now, with Sam on one side and the boys on the other, they lowered the coffin on two ropes. It came to a gentle rest, and the two brothers pulled the ropes slowly out from under while Sam stood with head bowed.

After a moment Sam said softly, "One thing from the Bible she liked. 'And Adam called his wife's name Eve; because she was the mother of all living.'" He paused, then continued, "For me, Nettie, you were the mother of all living. You were life itself." Raising his head, he said, "God. God, just one thing. Take care of this woman, Amen."

Clint and Pacer, Roslyn a step away, and Phillips still more distant, each said, "Amen," and the two sons reached for their shovels.

"No," Sam said. "Leave me alone. I'll fill."

The brothers dropped off their shovels in the barn and went into the house, where Roslyn and Phillips had gone.

"Will you eat?" Roslyn asked quietly. "You both need something."

Pacer took a long, soft breath and spoke for the first time since his father had returned with the lifeless figure in his arms. He stared at Phillips with tiny glints of pain and of rage moving deep in his dark eyes. "He's right."

"What?" Phillips said, unconsciously moving away from the younger brother.

"Clint was right. You killed her. You and those at The Crossing. Time wasted might have saved her."

Roslyn had left a sharp cutting knife on the table, and Pacer picked it up. He moved swiftly toward the doctor, who retreated in almost paralyzed fear, crying, "It's not my fault!"

Clint stepped between them and slammed Pacer's wrist

down, then pushed his brother back. "Stop it!"

Catching his balance, Pacer stood ready for another attack. "Move out of the way!" Suddenly his voice went higher. "Move! She was worth a thousand of all of them! White men shot her! They let her die!"

He charged again, and Clint's wrist was slashed as he met Pacer's attack. The older brother brought his left fist crashing around into the side of Pacer's head, and the heavy, fierce blow knocked Pacer down as the knife flew from his hand.

"It won't bring her back!" Clint half shouted.

Pacer grabbed the knife once more. "Don't try to stop me again!"

Phillips turned and ran from the door, and Clint kicked Pacer's legs out from under him as he rushed across the room. Roslyn stood still, her back against the wall, her eyes parted wide in fear, as the two brothers struggled savagely at the door, their sorrow turned for the moment to fury.

Twice the knife in Pacer's hand drew blood as he fought to get out. Once the point nicked Clint's jaw as the knife flew by his face, and once the blade sliced through jacket and shirt and into his upper left arm.

Hoofbeats sounded from the yard as Dr. Phillips, his heart pounding deafeningly in his own ears, rode into the night and back toward The Crossing.

Clint's great hand swept down and cracked against Pacer's knife arm so hard that his wrist should have been broken, and the younger brother dropped his weapon. Then Clint forced him back with swift, heavy, punishing blows to the head and chest. Near the center of the room, he struck Pacer's forehead with a long, nearly invisibly fast right fist, and Pacer fell back, tripped over a chair and cracked his head on the stone fireplace.

Picking the chair up and holding it as a club, Clint stood panting above his brother. Pacer was almost impossible to knock out, but his eyes were glazed, and he lay still for a moment.

Clint put the chair down and straddled it, his arms resting over the chair back. Breathing heavily, he said, "Best way to bust up a fireplace I ever saw."

Roslyn stepped toward them hesitantly and spoke in a thin voice. "You're both crazy. And you're bleeding, Clint. Let me—"

He shook his head. "It'll stop." His attention was all on Pacer. He understood his brother's feelings, and he knew a beating would not change his mind. "You okay?" he asked his younger brother in a low voice.

Pacer sat up slowly and, with his back to the fireplace, leaned his head on his arms, which were crossed over his drawn-up knees. He stayed bowed in silent thought for at least two full minutes. When at last he raised his eyes to look at Clint, the lines of fury and hate were still etched on his face. His eyes were no longer glazed or wild-looking, but they appeared as hard as the stones in the fireplace behind him.

"You ought to 've let me kill him," he said flatly.

Clint frowned and shook his head. "Pacer, no good could be done. It wouldn't help."

"I say it would. And all the others."

"Oh, God, Pacer!" Clint stood up and pushed the chair away from him.

"All the others at The Crossing that stood in our way!"

For the first time in his life, Clint couldn't get to his brother without words, and since he was so little used to working with words, they hindered him more than they helped. "That's plain foolish!"

"You know it's not!" Pacer stood up. "I want to see every man of them dead! Dead!" His eyes began to flare again.

"No, Pacer!" Clint groped for words. "You're talking like a—"

"Like a Kiowa!" Pacer finished for him in a low, deadly voice. "That's what Ma was. A Kiowa! That's why she's dead right now! That's what I am and what I'm damned well going to be!"

"Meaning what?"

"Meaning I'm going to ride with Buffalo Horn!" Without his wanting it to, his voice rose again so that it

86

became almost a cry. "Can't you see they killed our ma? Don't you care?"

"Don't ever put that question again!" Clint stepped forward angrily, then controlled himself. "But she wouldn't want more killings."

"She didn't know them like I do! She was out trying to stop the raids, trying to save their rotten hides, when they shot her and let her lay and die!"

Trying to shame his brother into better sense, Clint laughed suddenly and bitterly. "You join 'em then, you'll come against us when they hit our place?"

"That won't happen! You and Pa'll be all right."

"No!" Clint banged his hand flat on the table. "Only thing'll make Pa all right is for what's left of us to stay together."

Timidly, Roslyn spoke from where she stood in the center of the room. "Pacer, above all else, you're a civilized human being."

"I am not!" The younger brother wiped one hand over his face, finding a light film of cold sweat there. "Folks at The Crossing are civilized. That's not for me!" He glared at her with sudden, angry distrust. "Take yourself. I don't know what you thought of Ma. But I know what you think of me. It's all very fine to say that most of all I'm a human being. But ever since you've been old enough to know, you never looked at me without thinkin' somewhere back in your head, he's a Kiowa! Clint may be all right, but keep your eye out for Pacer!"

"That's not so!" Tears sprang to Roslyn's eyes as she faced him, and she knew that the tears were partly from angry humiliation because what he had said was so. "I always held you both the same."

Pacer stared at her, seeing the truth in the tears, and Clint said tiredly, "This is no night to carry on like this. Let's try to get some rest. We need it."

This didn't work, either. Pacer got his hat and put it on. Facing the bunks, his back to Clint, he said, "I said what I meant. Of all people, Clint, you should know I'm not joking."

The older brother crossed the room toward him and spoke softly. "I do know. And it's a concern to me." He paused. "A big concern, because you know I won't let you go out that door."

Pacer turned to face him. "Never a real fight in our life, and you plan to make two in the same night?"

"If need." :

"It needs be, then."

Clint spoke to Roslyn without taking his eyes off Pacer. "Go into the folks' bedroom, Roslyn. And shut the door."

When she had gone, silently obeying, he continued, "You know yourself bad things have been said about us for a long, long time. A crazy thing like you got in mind would just prove that everybody's been right all along."

"That's what I'm about to prove."

"Pa's the one to think about." Clint's voice choked under the strain of trying to be calm. "He's alive and needs us. Needs us more'n ever."

"Pa's a strong man. Will be till the day he dies. Ma was a little thing, helpless and easy hurt." Pacer leaned against the top bunk, shaking his head against the blankets. "If I prove Kiowa blood is poison, that's all right. Ma can't be hurt more, and I sure don't give a damn." He swung around to face his brother. "Two things, Clint. First, it was my fault taking her out there when I knew it wasn't right."

"No one ever held blame for you."

Pacer shook these words aside impatiently. "And second, maybe what other people think of a man helps him to become that. Don't know. But I do know I'm ready—more than ready—to go with Buffalo Horn." He took a long, slow breath. "As a personal favor, which I never made a point to ask you before, don't try to stop me."

Clint shrugged, but his body was tense and ready. "I can't do other."

Since his back was touching the top bunk, it gave Pacer a sort of springboard from which to shove out, and his right fist hit Clint directly on the point of the jaw, lashing

88

out with so much speed that Clint had no time to duck or roll with the blow.

Pacer hit him twice more in rapid succession, and the fight should have been over. But short of a concussion, neither of Sam's sons could be knocked unconscious. Clint grappled forward blindly and caught Pacer in his powerful arms, holding him from moving to the door of the house.

Pacer managed to tear himself loose, but by that time strength had flowed back into Clint and he pounded Pacer over the ear with a wildly thrown left fist that sped on by, almost unchecked, as the lighter man fell to the floor.

Clint dived at his brother to hold him down, but Pacer rolled swiftly to his left and only Clint's right arm caught him partially, and then he was back up on his feet and Clint was whirling, only half on his feet, toward the door.

Picking up a piece of wood from the fireplace, using it as a short, stout club, Pacer tried to pound his way through Clint's powerful defense. On his third swinging blow, Clint grabbed the piece of wood in mid-flight and wrenched it from his grip.

As the older brother started toward him, dropping the club, Pacer struck him once more, this time missing his chin and hitting his throat. Clint grunted in pain, and blood inched from the edges of his lips, but he came on, his fists slamming against Pacer like two, bone-and-flesh battering rams.

Falling back, realizing that he could not whip Clint with muscle and speed alone, Pacer retreated beyond Clint's punishing fists. He fumbled for a moment with the Joslyn in his belt, and then pulled it out.

Seeing the gun, Clint could not believe Pacer meant it and kept on coming.

Thumbing the hammer back swiftly, Pacer said coldly, "Stop, or I'll kill you!"

Hesitating, Clint muttered deep in his throat, "Put it away."

"I'm leaving! I'll shoot if you come on!"

Clint shook his head as though to clear it and to help his torn throat muscles. Then for the first time he became really angry. "If you can pull a gun on me, if you can cock it and talk like that, then go ahead and get the hell out and stay!" He gasped deeply for air. "If you can do those things, then maybe everybody else was right after all and it was me who was wrong!"

"Don't try again to stop me." Pacer circled the table, his Joslyn centered on Clint's broad chest, and opened the door by reaching behind him. In the next instant he was gone, and the door was shut behind him.

Clint did not go after him. He would have had to count on using a gun, and this he could not do. He sat at the table, drawing long, slow breaths, and after a time he heard hoofs pounding away into the night.

The door to the bedroom opened and Roslyn appeared. She said nothing, waiting for him to speak.

"He's gone," Clint told her at last. "He'll calm down and come back," he added, though he did not believe it himself. "Maybe you ought to turn in. Be morning soon."

Roslyn nodded and went back into the bedroom, too shaken by the events of the last hours to trust herself to speak.

When, sometime later, Sam came into the house, Clint said, "Roslyn's using the other room. Pacer rode out."

"I saw." Sam took off the jacket he'd been wearing and hung it neatly on the rack to one side of the fireplace. He was exhausted, and his sorrow seemed to have shriveled his spirit, for there was no power in him as he spoke. "Where'd he go?"

"Oh," Clint said, failing miserably at trying to be off-handed, "some stupid notion of throwing in with Buffalo Horn. He'll be back soon as he comes to his senses."

"Doubt it." Sam put his hands briefly to the low fire, wondering vaguely at the fact that he seemed not to feel the heat. "Can't say I blame him."

Clint looked at his father with surprise, and Sam said, "Things aren't cut and dried in this world, son. At times a wrong thing seems right, or a right thing wrong. And sometimes you just don't know which is which."

Clint knew that his father was hardly hearing or paying attention to his own words. In a sense, Sam looked as big and powerful as ever, yet his words and his very way of moving showed he was only a husk of his former self.

"Guess you're right, Pa."

"Odd." Sam finally moved his hands, deciding that they would never be warm again and that it didn't matter anyway. "When I first came out here, all those years ago, I had nothing but myself and you, Clint. And now, after the work Nettie and me put in, and all you and Pacer did to help as you grew fit and big enough, I'm back to where I started. I got myself. And I got you." He stepped to the table and laid a hand on Clint's shoulder. "The land gives. And the land takes." He stared at the glowing coals in the fireplace. "Must be the land as does it. Not God, like we're taught. God would most like have better sense than to give and then take in such a senseless manner."

CHAPTER THIRTEEN

Pacer rode through the darkness of Buckskin Pass and came to its western mouth when the grayest suspicion of dawn was moving into the sky behind him.

He rode to the place where Will Howard's insane attack had come and found the two bodies—Howard's and Two Moons'—lying where they had been left the night before. which seemed now like a lifetime ago.

Dismounting, he stared briefly at Howard's lifeless face. Then, with his right boot, he turned the body over twice, and on the third roll it flopped into a shallow ravine. A decent enough burial for the man, Pacer decided.

Two Moons' silver-dust stud had long since wandered off, while the warrior himself lay sprawled on his side. Since the scent of blood had evidently not been carried to the nostrils of scavengers, Two Moons had no marks upon him save the frightful wound that made his face unrecognizable.

Pacer lifted the warrior onto his own pony, quieting the animal with gentle words. Holding Two Moons' body draped across the horse, he stepped into the saddle and continued on his way toward the Kiowa camp.

The sun was still low in the after-dawn sky when he arrived at the outskirts of the village. Three riders rode forward to meet him, and after wordless stares at Two Moons, they fell in beside him as he went on into the camp.

Buffalo Horn was waiting in the center of the village a few paces from his tent. He spoke a short, curt command as the horse stopped near him, and two braves stepped close to the animal to lift Two Moons down.

Pacer swung out of the saddle and stood facing the chief. "You have lost one fighter and gained another."

Buffalo Horn nodded. "Who did this?"

"A white man. He also killed N'edd'ee-pahs, the woman who was my mother. That white man is now dead."

The chief closed his one eye for a moment. "My words mean nothing. But my spirit goes out to you." When the single, hard eye fastened on Pacer again, he added, "The white man is dead by your hand?"

"Yes."

"This is good. Your sorrow will be lessened by it."

Pacer saw a girl standing a few feet away in the crowd that had gathered, and though there were no tears in her eyes, her head was bowed and her face drawn into lines of grief. She glanced up at Pacer, and he read her face rightly and said, "You were to be the woman of Two Moons?"

She nodded, not speaking. She was a plump girl of about fifteen, with huge dimples that were exaggerated even further by her high, prominent cheekbones.

"He died as a warrior, moving fast and straight toward his enemy. But for bad fortune, he would have come back with a scalp."

Lame Crow and, a step behind him, Poh'sha-knay pushed their way through the crowd until they were near.

"This is a bad thing," Lame Crow said, "about Two Moons and my woman's sister."

Thinking of the harsh words that these two had said to his mother, Pacer said coldly, "First I was speaking of Two Moons, and now I look at you, Lame Crow. And I find it hard to say whether you or your woman is the greater warrior in your teepee."

Lame Crow glared at Pacer, but did not have either wit or courage to reply. He turned and walked away from the group, and his woman followed, silent and cowed as a dog might have been.

It was the quiet, timid Singing Hawk who picked up Two Moons' body to carry it away from the camp where it would be placed on poles lifting it closer to the northwest heaven. Other friends of Two Moons' fell in behind Singing Hawk.

Buffalo Horn said to Pacer, "If we have wisdom to see, out of all evil things good may come. You are with us. This is good. You will give us strength in many ways."

Pacer watched the Indians moving out toward the open, where Two Moons would be put to rest. "When we go into battle, I will think of my mother, and I will think of how Two Moons tried to help her. And I will be strong—very strong."

That morning, while Roslyn fixed breakfast, Clint took care of the chores. Sam was up earlier than either of them, after only one or two hours' sleep, but he did nothing besides build up the fire and sit at the table with sightlessly staring eyes.

After a spiritless breakfast of beef and potatoes, Roslyn washed the dishes at the cooking board while Clint saddled horses so that he could take her back to The Crossing.

He purposely left Roslyn's own horse in the corral, for it was still tired from the long, hard run it had made yesterday. When he led the horses to the house, Roslyn was ready.

She stood in the door, half turned toward the silent man still sitting at the table. Then she recrossed the room and said to him, "I'm sorry, Mr. Burton. So very sorry."

Sam shuffled to his feet, and in a moment he said in a thick, low voice, "I'm beholden for the sentiment, Roslyn, and for your coming here."

Then she was gone, hurrying from the room, and a few seconds later she and Clint were riding onto the sunlit, dew-speckled flats.

When the house was a faraway dot behind them, she said, "At The Crossing, I won't say anything about what Pacer had in mind. He'll be back."

"Maybe."

Roslyn swung about to look at Clint riding straight and seemingly tireless in the saddle near her. "He will change his mind. He couldn't do that."

"Don't know. He's been pushed a long way."

94

"If he has, then so have you. And your pa."

"That's so." Clint put his right hand up to where the knife had punctured his left arm. It was a shallow cut, and the bleeding had not been bad. He'd changed into his other shirt this morning. Now, putting his hand there had nothing to do with pain or concern for the wound. It was, rather, a gesture to convince himself that Pacer had really done this, that it was not a bad dream resulting from the death of his ma. It was hard to think that Pacer had fought him with killing weapons—yet it had happened.

"Yes, that's so. But Pacer, and Ma, had the hardest time. Me, I had the easiest. Different from Pa, I didn't marry a Kiowa woman. Different from Pacer, Kiowa blood wasn't in me." He lowered his hand once more so that it rested easily on the saddle horn, holding the reins loose. "People aren't too smart. They take a man for what they think he ought to be, not for what he is."

Several minutes went by in silent riding, and then, as they pushed through a narrow gully and on into the prairie stretching wide and desolate beyond, Roslyn said, "You've been taken for what you are. No questions asked. It's true for me, anyway. I've always judged you for what you were—for me you've always been a lot." She hesitated. "And Pacer, too."

"Oh? You recall when Pacer and me came to The Crossing, before we knew about the Howards? Remember what Angus said? Remember what you said?"

"But we were beside ourselves!"

"Somebody gets drunk enough, excited enough, and he sometimes says things that are the truest things he ever puts words to." Clint could see that Roslyn was upset. He added, "Doesn't matter."

"But it does matter!"

"What would you have me say?"

"I don't know. But I reach for you and reach for you, and you're not there!"

He said, "You reach for any man and he doesn't reach back, he's too dumb to waste yourself on."

During midday they arrived at the near outskirts of The Crossing. Before their horses reached the short stretch of

95

buildings that lined each side of the street, Dred and Angus Pierce hurried on foot to meet them. Each of the Pierce men carried a rifle.

"Get down offen that horse, Ros!" Dred commanded.

Tired and unhappy, the girl lashed back with sudden, angry words. "Don't talk to me like that! I'm a woman grown, Pa, and I'll leave you if you try to shame me!" She stayed on her horse.

Startled, Dred did not reply for a moment, and when he did, it was in a calmer voice and he knew he would never have complete authority over his daughter again. "While you been out goin' among the enemy, the Jenkins place was hit last night. How you feel about that?"

"They cut down Hal an' Phil," Angus said. "Them boys was out away from the house. Two good men gone, when we'll be needful of every good fightin' man around."

"If the two of you, and the others, weren't so unforgivably stupid," Roslyn said cuttingly, "you'd have the best three fighting men in this country lined up with you."

"Sure," Dred mumbled. "The kind as what goes around killin' and kidnapin' people." He flicked his hate-filled eyes over Clint, not daring to lock stares with him. "Doc says t'other one like to killed 'im last night."

Clint said nothing, having nothing to say to these men or anyone else in The Crossing. He'd stayed this long only to be sure Roslyn would not be ill-treated by the Pierce men.

He was about to rein his horse around when a small voice came to his ears. "Hey, Mister Clint!"

It was Maggie Phillips, who had come from her house toward them. As the little girl approached the horses, her mother appeared at the doorway and shouted in near panic, "Maggie! Get back here!"

"It'll be all right, ma'am," Dred called back. "Me an' my boy are lookin' out for her."

Clint's face went tight at Dred's remark, but he still said nothing.

Maggie drew near to his stirrup and, in a loud whisper that could be heard by all four of the adults, said, "When Pacer picked me up he made me lose a penny." She stuck

96

her hand into a pocket of her dress and wiggled the hand around loosely to prove her point. "You tell him he owes me a penny."

Clint stuck his hand into his own pocket and found just two cents there. He leaned down in the stirrup and handed them to the girl.

"Oh, thanks!" She seemed pleased for a moment but then her pleasantly puckered face turned thoughtful. As she started away she looked back and said without malice, "Pacer'd have give me a nickel!"

Roslyn watched the small, departing figure. "Pacer can be very generous."

Shifting to face the girl at his side, Clint said in what was almost a whisper, "Right there you hit it. You say he can be generous. You didn't say he is generous. And by saying he can be, you're sort of holding it a thing in his favor, as though at least there's that to be said for him."

He made a move to turn his pony, and Roslyn said desperately, "I said what I thought was a nice thing!"

He touched her arm lightly, then whirled his horse and rode away at a hard lope, wanting to put The Crossing as far behind him as possible.

Even the one person who tried the most, Roslyn, could not understand. Anyone who knew Pacer, if they had the sense to see, would know that he would cut off his right arm for you. You didn't down a man like that. Nor did you set him apart by trying to say the right thing about him, trying to build him up when such was not needed.

Just once Clint turned, and from two points in the spreading prairie that stretched far and wide in the slanting flats behind him, he saw wagons moving slowly into town—settlers coming in to be safe, risking the easy looting and burning of their deserted homes in exchange for their lives.

First the Howards. Now the Jenkinses. The feel of war was in the air.

CHAPTER FOURTEEN

Sam spent nearly an hour to himself and his unmoving loneliness after Clint and Roslyn left the house. It was when he at last reached out and touched his coffee cup and found that it was cold that he realized to some degree how long he had sat there at the table.

Moving wearily, he cleared the table of the few things Roslyn had left there for him. Then he went to the barn and began to fashion a wooden marker for his wife's grave. He did not want a simple cross, but rather one of the solid headboards with a curved top. Selecting a two-inch-thick piece of solid oak, he went to work slowly and carefully. By mid-afternoon it was finished and deeply imbedded in place at the head of the mounded dirt.

Aside from her name and the dates of her life, he could think of nothing more fitting to burn into the wood than the thing he had said the night before. And thus it was printed deep in the solid oak: "The Mother of All Living."

The five words made sense and were meaningful to Sam.

He saddled a horse and set out aimlessly to ride his land. Every rock and scrub brush and flower seemed different to him now that she was not there. Less colorful. Less vital. Less living.

After a time, almost without thought, he turned his pony southwest and headed for the box canyon in which he and Clint had put the cattle they had rounded up. Some of them would have wandered by now, would need hazing back into the natural hiding place.

The steers had not roamed much, still satisfied with the

grass and the clear stream that flowed down from a small, natural spring at the end of the short, boxed-in canyon. Half a dozen or so had wandered out a half mile onto the flat, though, and Sam rode out to head them back in.

He almost missed two head even farther out on the flat, seeing them only after he had ranged the first group into the massive, earthen walls that formed a protection against the eyes of enemies.

If he had not gone out after the steers, putting himself in sight for at least two miles across the flats, his life might have been saved.

There were nine warriors from the Ton-poh'-kah village that lay twelve days to the northeast. These Kiowa braves had been headed south and west to join the great, one-eyed chief Buffalo Horn, and they were just now very pleased with themselves. Two of their number carried fresh scalps, still damp to the touch, from their raid of the night before. These, and the few things they had taken from their victims—a watch, a revolver, a folding knife and something that made a musical noise when you blew into it—would be fine mementos of their skill and courage as fighters and would do much to impress Buffalo Horn and those already with him.

They were now headed almost due west, scouting the mountains before them for the easiest way to cross, when they saw the lone rider come out of the moutains to the right of them and far away.

At a signal from their leader, they dropped out of sight behind a slanting hill.

One of them felt that there might be more enemies where the one rider had come from, and he believed that they would do well to let their success of the night before stand. "We have two scalps, and none of us is hurt. The gods have been good to us, but maybe they won't be if we are too greedy."

But he was an older, cautious brave, and the others agreed with a young, bold man who said, "The gods are making us a gift of that enemy. We would be spitting in their faces if we went away."

Preoccupied with one of the steers, a bullheaded white-face with one horn turned up and the other turned down, which wanted nothing less than to go back into the box canyon, Sam was not aware of the Kiowas for a long time. Separated and riding stealthily, hiding where they could as they came up on him, they were almost in arrow range before he turned around, warned by instinct, perhaps by a sight or sound or smell so slight that it alerted him without his being conscious of it.

He saw a painted face disappear as a brave in a gully behind him leaned far down over his horse's neck.

But the Indian realized surprise was now lost, even as he leaned down, and he yelled to inform the others. Nine shrieking Indians charging out of cover in a half-mile semicircle would have seemed at a moment's glance and hearing to be the entire Kiowa nation, but Sam instantly judged them to be about ten, even as he put heels to his pony and raced in the only direction he could go—straight back toward the box canyon.

Sam had no time to wonder why he suddenly felt good and free, young and strong at a time like this. If there had been time, he would have judged correctly that great danger was the only thing that could take his mind off Ma. His sorrow had been an insidious enemy, coming from inside where it cuts a man's strings, making useless the outside defenses a man builds up and keeps intact. But these savages were an outside enemy that a man could deal with on a man's terms, could hope to conquer if he had enough skill and power.

As the two Kiowas armed with guns sent lead slugs singing past him, it was almost with relief and pleasure that Sam took the big Colt dragoon from his side and turned around to fire at them.

His third shot caused one of the Indians to go loose in body and slide off his galloping pony's back. As Sam charged into the canyon, the steers were now bawling nervously at the explosions, beginning to mill in tight circles that might erupt into a stampede at any moment.

Realizing this, the Kiowas split up as they came into the

mouth of the canyon, not wanting to be caught in a madly charging wall of cattle.

Sam was on the south side of the herd, and for a brief instant he thought of deliberately breaking the herd out and riding for cover with it.

He never found out if the plan might have worked. A chance shot snapped by one of the rifle-armed Kiowas shattered his horse's leg. The animal swept into a whinnying dive on the slanting canyon slope and Sam was thrown over its head.

Sam's thoughts were those of a natural fighting man. Given his present situation in a puzzle, it might have taken him two hours to come up with the best possible solution. Yet now, even before he hit the ground he knew what to do. He landed on his shoulder and was up on his feet and running with the roll of his spill, sprinting toward the nearest steer with the idea of catching a ride and roaring out with the forming stampede.

Before him there was a drop of about eight feet he had to jump down. It was not high enough, and there wasn't time enough, to make it a two-footed jump. He landed on one foot, intending to take it in stride. It was his game leg, and the leg crumpled under him.

He whirled, gun still in hand, as the first Indian rider slanted down the eight-foot bank on his pony, and Sam shot the Kiowa twice.

The rumbling herd began spilling out of the canyon in gathering terror as the other four warriors on Sam's side of the slope charged down the embankment. His last shot with the dragoon missed fire, and he said, "Damn!" softly as the four circled him warily, shooting arrows into him.

The three Kiowas on the far side now rode through the settling dust clouds left by the stampeding cattle and joined those dismounting near Sam, who lay, leg folded under him, face down.

"It was expensive," the older warrior said, looking at the big, crumpled body with four arrows jutting from it.

The bold young brave said, "He was lucky," and stepped toward Sam with his scalping knife drawn.

Before Sam allowed the life to go out of him, as the arrows pounded into his body, he swore again at the last cartridge that had misfired. The dragoon was under him, almost nestled against his throat, and his fingers still clutched it. Counting very slowly and carefully, he worked the cylinder around one chamber less than a full cycle.

He was aware, as if it were happening in another world, that new riders had come up and were sitting their horses near him. And then he felt rough fingers in his hair.

Twisting his head, opening his eyes one last time, he was surprised to find that he was blind in his left eye. But through his right he could see dimly, and so he saw the look of astonishment that came over the Kiowa's face as the hammer of the dragoon came down once more and this time did not misfire.

A hole appeared in the brave's chest, high up, and he sat down suddenly. He died at the same moment that Sam—old Stonewall—Burton let the last bit of life go out of his own body.

It was late that night before the six remaining braves from the Ton-poh'kah village arrived at Buffalo Horn's camp. They had argued at length about the foolishness or wisdom of having attacked that last, lone white man, and whether the gods were for or against them now. They had gone too far north in their search for the Kiowa camp.

Therefore, they rode in from the north, and seemed to have come from a direction which would never have placed them anywhere near Flaming Lance.

They boasted about their great battle—not mentioning that there had been two of them—and told of one great giant of a man who had had magical power to stay alive. Yet even so they had at last conquered him, with some small loss.

Such boasting was typical Kiowa fighting talk, and a reasonable listener always subtracted about three feet of height from the giants any braves had encountered, giants who often seemed nine feet tall.

Sitting next to Buffalo Horn when the Ton-poh'kah warriors showed the three scalps they had taken, Pacer glanced at the war trophies without interest. Except for a

102

victim with strikingly colored hair, any scalp was pretty much like another.

Pacer had something more important on his mind: revenge. Revenge for what had been done to his mother, and for the tragedy it had brought into Pa's, Clint's and his lives.

CHAPTER FIFTEEN

Clint arrived at Flaming Lance at twilight, and was not surprised to find that his father was not there. He considered starting supper for himself and Pa, but decided against it. Not wanting food, but knowing he would soon lose strength without it, he cut a chunk of beef from the meat Roslyn had cooked. Eating with one hand, sometimes holding the meat between his teeth when both hands were needed, he took care of his winded horse and tossed the saddle onto a big, fresh blue roan.

When he rode out to track Pa, almost all light was gone. He followed Sam's trail to the north briefly, passing Ma's grave closely enough to make out the lettering by squinting through the gathering dark.

But north was not right, and he felt this within him. There was no reason for Pa to ride north, beyond a simple look-see at his land. Once on horseback, Clint was certain, Pa would have gone to his cattle sooner or later.

So giving up the trail which would be soon lost to him anyway, he swung left and back at an angle to head straight for the box canyon. The Evening Star glinted over the peaks ranging north and south to his right as he lost sight of the house in the dark and distance behind him.

Long before he came to the canyon the moon was casting the color of milk over the flats, and as he drew still closer, his stomach tightened for a reason he did not understand for a long moment.

Then he knew that it was too quiet. Even from out here, and given that the cows had bedded for the night, he should be hearing an occasional, far-away bawling. A crying calf or a steer complaining—these were things that kept any herd from ever being totally quiet for very long. And he judged he had been in hearing range for three or four minutes by now.

At the mouth of the canyon, already knowing the herd was gone, he made out the sound of low, angry growls that were an almost whispered argument between two coyotes. Staring hard into the dark gray shadows of the canyon, he saw the beasts crouched over a dim figure that did not look at all like a downed steer. As the scavengers ripped and tore at the flesh before them, heedless of his approach until too late, he pushed his pony up the canyon with his drawn gun in hand.

His first shot sent one of the coyotes spinning back and away from the dim figure, yipping and howling in pain, snapping blindly at the air. Its mate whirled and rushed away up the side of the canyon. Clint's second shot missed, but his third brought the last coyote down with a foreleg nearly blown off, and his fourth bullet pounded solidly into the animal's body.

Clint swung down before his horse had come to a complete stop.

Even in the dusky, silver-toned darkness, the story was easy to read.

There were six arrows in Pa, and a rifle slug had gone into his left wrist. No two of the arrows had been made by the same warrior, nor had the shafts been withdrawn for future use, which was a tribute to Pa, meaning he had not been easy killed. The coyotes had not been at him long, for which Clint was grateful as he turned his father onto his back and saw that the face was whole, but he winced when he saw that Pa had been scalped.

The big dragoon Colt was still clutched in Pa's right fist—a further sign of respect for a fearful warrior.

Clint pried the gun loose and jammed it into his belt. Quieting the big blue roan in a calm voice that did not betray the unnatural dryness in his eyes, Clint pulled the arrows from his father, then hefted Sam's body onto the wide-eyed, nervous roan. He tied the body in place, stomach across the saddle, wrists and feet bound with a length of lariat running next to the girth around the horse's belly.

Going home, he led the roan instead of riding. The horse was a big-chested, powerful animal, one of the fastest mounts in the Flaming Lance remuda. Clint did not want to tire it or strain it with the weight of two big men. He would be needing a good, fast horse, and in his mind he'd already settled on the roan.

When he had lighted candles and laid his pa out on the bed where his mother had so recently lain in death, Clint noticed for the first time a small patch of powder burn on Sam's jacket collar. A gun had been fired with its barrel placed almost flush along his father's throat.

Odd, that, and Clint did not know what it meant. He did not need to. He knew there had been at least seven Kiowas. He knew that some of them had been carried away to be placed on poles or, if the Indians were in a hurry, to be buried under piles of rocks. He knew this even without the signs left by Kiowas to tell a knowing person of a hard fight—for he knew his father.

It took most of the night for Clint to bury his pa. Working for the second night by the yellow gleam of the kerosene lamp, he at last lowered the crude coffin with a dull thump into the grave beside his mother's. There was nothing to say, and no one to say it, so he stood briefly with his hat off and thought of all the things that might have been said of his pa had there been anyone there to listen to the words or to understand them.

Clint was not sure what to put on the headstone he made, duplicating his mother's.

Again, there was so much, and so little, to say. So he took the heated iron and printed simply:

SAM BURTON
1831-1881

It was almost daylight when Clint went into the house, and he had never been so tired in his life. Bolting the door and battle shutters, he lay on his bunk fully clothed, mean-

106

ing to rest for a few minutes. He closed his eyes for a moment, and when he reopened them he could tell by the slanting light at the windows that the sun was high up in the sky.

Though he had not wanted to waste time with sleep, he knew it was the best thing to do. He would need all his strength. After eating more of the beef without tasting it, he saddled the rested and well-fed roan and brought it to the house.

He took four guns—his own Colt, Pa's dragoon, his Henry repeating rifle and the double-barreled shotgun. The dragoon he jammed into his belt, where he'd carried it the night before, and the shotgun he lashed behind the cantle where it would be easy to get in hand. Then he pointed his roan west toward Buckskin Pass to kill a man he'd never really seen or spoken to—Buffalo Horn.

Though Clint did not think too deeply into his reasons, acting purely on emotional intelligence, which is often the greatest wisdom, he was dimly aware that his pa was only part of his reason.

The Kiowas and the whites at The Crossing could have wiped each other out and he would not have lifted a gun to help either side. Dred and Angus Pierce, Ben Ford, Phillips and the others meant nothing to him beyond a dull hatred. But there were others at The Crossing—Roslyn and the little girl, Maggie. The other children
. . .

Clint took the road across the mountains edging the pass rather than riding through the easy way. Keeping clear of the higher ridges, he was less likely to be seen or ambushed, and he could see farther from these upper levels.

There was nothing to see.

Clint came down the lowering foothills and rode by the place where his mother had been shot. Six or eight big death-black buzzards were flapping clumsily about in a shallow gully a few yards away.

He guessed that would be Will Howard, but he did not ride close or do what he would have normally done—blast into the ugly, ghoulish birds with the shotgun. He would not chance a shot, nor would he risk a keen, distant eye spotting a buzzard flapping excitedly into the air.

He rode on, not knowing where the big Kiowa camp was, but knowing he would find it.

An hour later he was on the crest of a rolling hill covered with scrub oak. The countless, twisted and gnarled branches around him would keep him from being easily spotted, and from here his hard, steady eyes swept patiently over the horizon, looking for the faintest suspicion of smoke that might mark the Indian camp.

It was from here that he first saw so much dust that for a moment he actually took it for smoke. The dust clouded up out of an arroyo more than a mile away, and after a long minute Indian riders began pouring out of the mouth of the arroyo.

Clint slipped out of his saddle and quickly tied the open-end reins together to loop around his arm, leaving both hands free. He pulled the Henry out of its saddle holster and cocked the rifle, waiting now unmoving in the protection of the thick scrub oak.

He knew Buffalo Horn was the big Kiowa on the lead horse. His position in the line of horsemen, his buffalo-horn headdress, his very bearing marked him as the leader of these men. And Clint realized it would take a strong man to lead so many of the naturally independent, rebellious Kiowas. There were at least forty of them strung out in a long sometimes doubled-up line. Clint saw that the rider nearest Buffalo Horn was Pacer.

Most of the warriors were riding second-best horses, leading their top war horses on short, rawhide lines, and this fact alone would have told Clint that the Kiowas were intent on a big, important attack where they would want their best horses as fresh and strong as possible.

As the rumble of hoofs came closer, bearing in the direction of Buckskin Pass, Clint could now make out the short, deadly war lance that Buffalo Horn carried and the scalps that hung from it.

Clint slowly raised the Henry in his arms and sighted through the open buck sights, and a terrible thought came to him. Did Pacer know about Pa, or, worse, could he have taken part in the attack on him? Clint forced the thought from his mind and returned to the simple problem of the moment, the killing of Buffalo Horn.

The chief was now no more than two hundred yards away and down from him, and Clint could place a shell within a two-inch square at that distance. He knew his own chances of living five minutes after his first shot were negligible, so it was necessary to make that shot count—a head shot, rather than a body shot from which Buffalo Horn might conceivably recover.

The chief's head, swaying with the rhythm of his pony's movements, appeared in the sights, and Clint tracked him briefly. Then he squeezed the trigger.

Clint never knew why he missed that shot.

Buffalo Horn knew. A piece of leather inside the band of his horned bonnet was loose and rubbing irritatingly against his temple. He bent his head, starting to bring his hand up to reset the bonnet, and it suddenly felt as though he'd been hit lightly with a club. One of the horns on his bonnet was shattered by the bullet.

It was then, a brief instant later, that he heard the bang of the rifle from the hill to his right.

Clint was back in his saddle, his head now showing above the scrub oak, as the outraged Kiowas came out of their surprised shock.

Not a chief to send others ahead of him, Buffalo Horn roared a furious command for the others to split up and go around the sides of the hill as Clint disappeared beyond the crest of the big, brush-covered mound. Then he himself galloped straight up the side of the hill toward where the white man had disappeared from sight.

The warriors split into two groups and thundered around each side of the hill to catch the enemy as he descended on the far side.

Clint, just over the rim, pulled his roan to a stomping halt, waited for a slow count of seven, and then charged right back over the hill.

As the clinging, tearing branches grabbed at his clothes, he jerked the shotgun from behind the cantle. Rac-

109

ing over the crest, he saw Buffalo Horn not more than thirty feet ahead of him. Pacer was twenty feet farther down the scrub-covered slope.

The Kiowa chief made a magnificent figure thundering up the slanting hill, arm flashing back with upraised lance as he suddenly saw Clint bearing down on him.

The shotgun boomed as Buffalo Horn's arm shot forward. Except for the weight of scalps on the lance, Clint might have died then. As it was, the lance hit him high up on the thigh, going in deep before it was ripped away by passing branches, leaving the thigh brutally torn open.

From the chest up, Buffalo Horn's body and face became unrecognizable, and he was tossed violently backward off his horse.

Pacer had his Joslyn in hand. He did not point it at Clint, and Clint gave him no chance to change his mind. The younger brother had pulled his mount to a side-turned halt, and Clint drove the big blue roan at full speed into the smaller horse under Pacer.

The smaller horse's hind quarters went out from under it, and it went sprawling onto the ground, whinnying in hurt and fear, as the blue roan bolted on down the slope.

Pacer was thrown clear, and as he hit the ground he saw that his own horse's left hind leg was broken. He ran a few quick steps to Buffalo Horn's big mare and leaped up, jerking the mare around and slapping her into a gallop back down the hill.

Now at the foot of the slope, Clint ran almost head-on into two Kiowa braves racing back around. He jerked back the offside hammer of the shotgun, and as the weapon boomed a second time, the first of the two warriors disappeared from his mount. With no time to pull another gun, Clint shifted the shotgun to clubbing position, barrel in hand. The second Kiowa, his horse still moving, hauled back swiftly on his bow string. The arrow sped into Clint's arm after he'd started his swing, but he brought the shotgun butt down on the Kiowa's skull, caving it in. The butt shattered under the impact, and Clint dropped the broken shotgun.

The blue roan's head stretched out, now that he was on

110

the flat, and he ran with every bit of muscle and heart in him. The arrow in Clint's right arm didn't send pain to his mind, but it seemed a silly, awkward thing that might get in the way, so he gave the horse its head and pulled off the loose, blood-smeared tip, then jerked the shaft out of his arm and threw it to the ground. With his usable left hand he pulled a bandanna from his hip pocket and tried to tie a knot that would stop the bleeding, but somehow the bandanna fell from his hold and went fluttering down to drape itself on a sagebrush top.

Clint knew the country ahead, and he knew that he had about a mile-and-a-half run before he would hit a long stretch of wild, broken land where he might lose his pursuers. A simple ride with a fair start, yet the badlands seemed to be taking a hellishly long time to appear. He saw the Widow's Chair, a low, misshapen butte that marked the beginning of the twisted, chopped-up country, but the butte seemed to be coming closer at a maddeningly slow rate, as if in a dream. He realized now that he should have slept longer this morning.

Glancing behind him, he saw in the distance so many riders that it was ludicrous that they should all be chasing him. The corners of his lips edged up faintly, and he murmured to himself, "There's only fifty thousand of 'em."

One of them was much closer to him than the others.

And then the ground leaped up as Clint turned back around on the blue roan, and the earth crashed against him.

Pacer was well ahead of the Kiowa warriors, and he was increasing his lead constantly on Buffalo Horn's powerful mare. Yet even so, Clint's blue roan ahead was holding his lead beyond Pacer. Clint had chosen his horse well.

The younger brother's quick eyes darted down at the land stretching ahead. He saw an almost unending wet trail of brown in the sand and dust, and he knew his brother would bleed to death soon at the rate that blood was gushing from him.

About half a mile from the badlands, Pacer saw Clint

111

wobble uncertainly in the saddle and, leaning out too far, go sprawling onto the ground. By sheer, unconscious instinct, Pacer believed, Clint somehow held onto the reins of the roan, and the animal came to a stomping halt after dragging its rider over a few feet of prairie.

Pacer had his belt in his hand long before he got to the roan and the downed horseman. An old Army-issue belt, it was the kind that stays tight under the pressure of the buckle itself at any point.

Bringing the chief's mare to such a rough halt that he risked breaking its jaw, Pacer flung himself to the ground and saw that the blood was coming mostly from the huge tear in Clint's thigh caused by Buffalo Horn's lance. He whipped the belt high around Clint's leg and hauled the end through the buckle, swiftly and rock-tight.

Clint was still faintly conscious, and he said, "Ow! That's a sure way to kill me."

Pacer heaved him onto his feet and almost threw him into the saddle. "Can you hold on?"

"Try to." Clint wrapped his big hands around the pommel.

An arrow made a noise that sounded like Whap! as it buried itself deep into the hind quarters of Pacer's mare. The animal reared violently, striking with its fore hoofs.

Pacer whirled, Joslyn in hand, and shot the Kiowa brave who was bent low over his horse's neck, stringing another arrow.

Then he was on the mare, leading Clint's roan, and surging into a full gallop as the shrieking Kiowas bore down on them.

An arrow split one of the mare's upraised ears in front of Pacer as bullets and whispering shafts hurtled about them. The Indians were so close that a thrown lance buried itself in the earth in front of the mare, and she shied so violently she almost tore the reins from Pacer's right hand leading the roan. Then they were rushing away swiftly, gaining against the Kiowas once more with their two heavier horses.

They circled Widow's Chair Butte far ahead of the Indians and galloped into a tangled land of arroyos, gullies and rock bluffs.

Once lost among these wildly shaped walls and slanting paths, Pacer deliberately slowed the horses and rode where he could through stone- or pebble-filled gullies so that they would not leave an easily followed trail. After winding and twisting through the maze for perhaps twenty minutes, he found a big, nearly hidden niche in the rocks and rode into it.

He jumped down and helped Clint from the saddle, laying him on the ground gently. "You still with me?"

Clint managed to shrug a little. "Latest count I was still alive." He was breathing hard. "Thanks for the lift back there."

Pacer took a canteen from Clint's saddle and gave him water, holding his head up for him. "You muddied the whole flat out there with your bleeding."

"That Buffalo Horn had a good arm on him."

Pacer said shortly, "A good man."

Since Clint thought they would probably not be alive much longer anyway, he decided to say nothing about Pa. Nor did he suggest that Pacer leave him and try to escape alone, for he knew that his brother would not.

The younger brother threw his hat on the ground and climbed one of the twenty-foot-high, nearly straight walls almost surrounding them. When he scrambled back down, he said, "They've broken up and are looking around, some afoot. Getting kind of close."

"Another two hours before nightfall," Clint said. "Bound to flush us out before then." He looked at the belt high around his leg. The bleeding had almost completely stopped. He tried to summon his strength, but weakness was the only thing he could discover. He tried to sit up and could not.

Pacer, fully realizing his brother's condition, began unbuttoning his shirt. "Maybe they won't flush us. Too many to fight. Maybe we can fool 'em." He dropped the shirt beside the hat on the ground. And standing before Clint in only his boots and khaki-colored denims, he reloaded the

113

spent cylinder in his Joslyn, then took Clint's Henry from the saddle holster on the roan.

And now Clint realized what his younger brother was thinking. Straight and lithe, his shoulders suggestive of tireless power and quickness, with his dark-toned skin and almost black eyes and black hair, Pacer could be mistaken briefly for a Kiowa warrior. At a glance, even his khaki-colored britches might be mistaken for dirty buckskin.

Clint said just one thing: "Your hair's too short."

Pacer nodded. "Might be a lot shorter pretty quick."

And then he was gone, silent and swift as any Indian warrior.

CHAPTER SIXTEEN

Pacer moved at a fast, crouching run until he was well away from where he had left Clint and the horses. Then he circled wide and came in behind several of the Kiowas who were searching closer and closer to the hiding place.

For a brief time he was clearly visible to them, at a distance of about a hundred yards. At least two of the braves saw him as he hurried across the open space. He ignored them. They paid no attention to him beyond a cursory glance.

Running down a narrow, winding gulch, Pacer at last came to a place far away from where the Kiowas were searching. He drew his Joslyn and fired twice, then cut loose with the Henry three times spacing the shots so that it sounded like a fight.

As he rushed away, there was a wild whoop from closer than he'd believed a Kiowa to be. And as he sped back along another arroyo, he heard dozens of voices as the braves rushed toward the scene of action.

Some distance away, he squeezed into a narrow cleft in a rock and reloaded his guns. The Kiowas were practically tearing the rocks apart where he had shot the five shells, searching angrily for the fight they had expected.

Someone found the three spent cartridges from the Henry, and there was a long involved conversation as various braves tried to explain their presence there.

"There are no horse tracks here! They would not give up their horses."

"They could not be behind us!"

"But they were! None of us carries a gun that shoots bullets like these."

115

"If those two were shooting, who was shot at? No one was shot at!"

"Maybe this place is haunted," a sober voice considered. "Let's act like this never happened."

Those first shots gained Pacer nearly half an hour. And during the next twenty minutes the warriors went back to their searching.

Twice men on horseback rode quickly past him, within a few yards. He knew in each case he had been seen, but each time the hoofbeats gave him enough warning to duck and search the ground, or turn so his face was not clearly visible.

Once, climbing a rock for a better view of what was going on, he raised his head over the top at the precise moment that another brave came over the far side of the rock, about thirty feet away. Pacer dropped back down quickly, raising his rifle in a quick, friendly wave, and hurried back down the tall slanting stone. The other brave, whom Pacer had not recognized, evidently suspected nothing and did not look at the rifle closely enough to recognize it as a Henry.

Skirting the back edges of the advancing searchers, Pacer squinted into the setting sun and gave the dark shortly more than an hour to arrive.

Seconds later, in a narrow arroyo, he almost collided with two of the Ton-poh'kah braves afoot. And one of them noticed his boots.

Pacer saw the man's face lift questioningly to his, and in that moment Pacer shot him point-blank.

The other brave whirled, his arm arching up with a war ax and slashing quickly down. Pacer had no time to lever a fresh shell into the breech. He raised the rifle with both hands and caught the descending ax across the barrel, at the same time raising one foot and kicking the Kiowa away from him. The Ton-poh'kah Kiowa screamed an enraged warning to the others in hearing. Pacer shot him, then ducked away and out of the arroyo.

Neither of the braves lived long enough to explain the mystery to their bewildered companions.

But this time there were dead men. There was no question of who had been shot at—although one warrior now put forth the suggestion that their two enemies could turn themselves into birds at will, to be able to fly from place to place.

Absolutely certain—unless the bird theory were true, in which case they were helpless anyway—that the two men were within shooting range of where the Ton-poh'kah braves had died, the Kiowas searched that area with painstaking care, even hitting the large rocks with smaller stones to make sure the rocks were not hollow.

The sun was down and light was fading when Pacer started back to where Clint and the horses were. He had gone only a few, quick steps when he ran into an unfamiliar warrior at a bend in the arroyo. And a step behind the strange warrior was Singing Hawk.

Pacer never knew if Singing Hawk intended to give him away or not. He gave himself away by trying to avert his face and hurry away. He did not want to fight Singing Hawk, the brave who had spoken perhaps two words in the years that Pacer had known him.

As he turned quickly, the other Indian said in thick, northern Kiowan, "What is the other with you?" This man was armed with a rifle, and he said, "Stop or I'll shoot!"

Pacer spun around and snapped off a shot before the other man had his gun up. Singing Hawk reached for the man's rifle as he fell, and, not knowing whether he intended to use it or not, Pacer shot him, too.

The other warriors were some distance away as far as Pacer knew, and he took the time to kneel over the dying Singing Hawk. "I'm sorry, I'm sorry!" he muttered brokenly.

Singing Hawk died as he had lived, without words. He raised his hand and touched Pacer's shoulder, gently and without reproach. His lips moved, though no sound came, and he nodded his head weakly just before he died.

Pacer hesitated a moment before running on, and in that moment the northern Kiowa behind him stabbed him in the back. It was a weakened, glancing blow, but the knife was sharp, and Pacer's back and part of his side were sliced open.

He got up and ran on toward the hiding place, not knowing that the knife wielder lived long enough to whisper to the warriors surrounding him a few seconds later, "Don't be fooled by the half-Kiowa again. He is almost naked and moving among us."

Clint had struggled to his feet once to quiet the horses as the Indian ponies drew near, and his efforts had started the bleeding again in his leg. He had, despite his complaint about Pacer's rough treatment, managed to pull the belt even tighter before he passed out briefly. He was still in a semiconscious state when his brother rushed into the now darkly shadowed niche.

"If we can ever make it," Pacer whispered, "it will be now." He hauled Clint up and lifted him once more to the saddle. A few seconds later they were moving quietly through the twisted, narrow walls, away from the Kiowa warriors.

Pacer led the roan up on the flat finally and pushed the mare into a lope, although the arrow in her hind quarters was beginning to lame her. Still, he did not dare pull the shaft. The arrowhead would stay in her anyway, and the additional bleeding caused by pulling the shaft might weaken her much more than the pain.

At Buckskin Pass, Pacer did the same thing that Clint had done earlier in the day. He followed the ridges up instead of riding straight through. At the highest point, he turned to study the prairie to the west, and in the faint light of the waning moon he thought he saw specks of solid black movement far out and away.

"They know where we came out of those badlands. They're following us."

Clint did not have the strength to turn in the saddle to look. His chest pushed against the pommel and his head rested on the roan's mane. "How far?" he asked.

"Hard to say. Five, six miles. Not moving too fast."

Pacer led off again, this time at a punishing speed that left Buckskin Pass quickly behind them.

As they approached the darkened house at Flaming Lance, Pacer said, "Where's Pa?"

118

Clint wanted to lie to him, but he could find no believable lie to put tongue to, and he said as they pulled up before the corral, "Pa's dead." He tried to swing out of the saddle, but he was so weak that he was able only to shift his weight before falling to the ground.

Pacer held him in a sitting position, his arms cradling Clint's head. "How'd Pa die?" Pacer asked.

"Kiowa raiders. Don't know what ones."

After a while Pacer said, "Well, I got the same thing to do either way. Was kind of hoping Pa'd be here to take you on into The Crossing."

"You know he wouldn't have gone off like that. He'd stay and fight."

"Yes. You're right. Lie still."

Pacer lowered his brother's head gently to the ground, then in the dark corral he found Roslyn's horse, which was used to being fed and sheltered at The Crossing. He tossed the saddle from the blue roan onto Roslyn's mount and cinched it tight, then bridled him.

Clint saw what was happening and objected with all the pathetically small power in him. "What you doin'? This is our home! I ain't going no place!"

It was harder for Pacer to heft Clint this time, for his own loss of blood was making itself felt. But he got Clint up. Then he cut short lengths of rope from the lariat on the saddle horn and lashed Clint's feet to the stirrups, both hands to the pommel.

The older brother could do nothing but lean powerlessly into the horse's mane, but he said as harshly as he could, "You're coming!"

Pacer left Clint's Colt in its holster, but he took the dragoon and he kept his own Joslyn and the Henry he'd been carrying. "No. I'm going back to the pass."

He slapped the horse viciously across the rump with a length of rope still in his hand and yelled "Wa-hooo!" at the frightened animal, sending it back toward The Crossing at top speed.

Not bothering with a saddle, he switched the single-rein bridle on Buffalo Horn's mare to a good-sized sorrel in the corral and swung up on the horse.

He rode full gallop to the pass and waited, hidden behind a rock at the eastern end.

He had been there only a few minutes when he heard the Kiowa riders coming through the dark shadows of the pass toward him.

CHAPTER SEVENTEEN

When Clint woke up, the first thing he did was to test his strength, which he had never realized was so dear to him. He clenched his fist, wherever it was in the dark vagueness about him, and the fingers had a little power—much more than they had had in his terrible dreams.

As his eyes focused, he saw that he was in a strange place, a plain, tidy room, and that Roslyn was standing over him.

When he had strength enough to speak, he said, "Where are we?"

She said nothing.

"What place is this?"

She remained silent, and he raised himself a little and almost shouted, "Tell me!"

"You're in my room," she said, trying to keep her voice calm. "My horse brought you in last night nearly dead."

Slowly, certain facts assembled themselves in Clint's mind. Roslyn's room was on the second floor of the Pierce store, and the Pierce store was in The Crossing.

Pacer!

Pacer was back at the pass, engaged in a hopeless battle.

He said, "My clothes?"

She nodded to a chair near him. "They're cleaned and iron—fixed up."

"Get out."

"You shouldn't move!"

But he had already thrown the blankets aside, and she began to retreat from the room, still pleading, "You should stay—"

"You think I'd stay here?" Weak as it was, his voice had a hard, cutting edge to it. "How long's it been now?"

"More'n twelve hours," she replied, speaking over her shoulder as he pulled on his shirt. "You like to died, Clint. Phillips fixed you up, an' I've been forcing broth down you—"

Clint glanced at the clean, white bandages on his arm and his thigh and for a moment was tempted to rip them off. He fought down the desire and pulled on his britches, walking barefoot to the window as he buttoned them, figuring the time of day by the slant of light outside. He was pulling on his boots when Dred Pierce came to the door.

"Feelin' some improved, Clint?"

"Who cares?"

Dred hesitated, "Why, me—an' everybody around here."

"Why?" The bitterness in Clint's tone had changed subtly to simple scorn.

"Well, a peaceful Tonkawa come through last afternoon an' said this town was doomed, so countin' for big talk even, we figured to be in for a fight. Never come. Flaming Lance is the only place between here and the Wild Tribes country—an' since you come in hurt an' all, we figured you somehow stopped 'em for us."

Clint shrugged into his jacket. "Me alone?"

"Uh-huh."

Clint crossed to the door, his injured leg barely holding his weight, as he buckled on his revolver. "Get out of the way or I'll kill you where you stand."

"Clint!" Roslyn gasped. "Him and Angus carried you up here last night in their arms!"

Clint brushed by the slighter man and started down the stairs. Angus stood on the lower floor, and he opened his mouth to speak, then shut it again as he saw the look in Clint's eyes.

Clint got to the door, leaned against the frame a brief moment to gather his strength, and then went out into the street. He started toward Ben Ford's blacksmith shop to

122

get a horse. He had gone about three steps when someone across the street near Phillips' house yelled, "A rider comin' in! Indi'n!"

Turning, Clint saw the lone rider, and though he could not at that distance make out Pacer's features, he knew the sorrel horse belonged to the Flaming Lance remuda.

Moving as fast as he could on his weak leg, Clint went out to meet his brother.

Pacer saw him coming and, with a slight, almost awkward tug at the reins, brought his horse to a halt.

From afar, Clint could see the dreadful wounds inflicted on his brother. Pacer was still hatless and naked to the waist. The left side of his face was clotted with dried blood, and as he drew closer Clint saw the jagged wound running along the left side of Pacer's head, from which blood had flowed. It looked as though someone had actually started to take his brother's scalp and had failed.

Deep, bloody wounds covered Pacer's body, and there was a bluish puncture in one side of his stomach that was the mark of a bullet hole. The younger brother's left arm had been gashed deeply from the shoulder to the elbow, and there was a rawhide thong tied tightly near the shoulder that Pacer must have somehow tied with one hand and his teeth.

As Clint approached him, Pacer pulled the sorrel away with his one good hand and said, "Don't come too close."

"What?" Clint whispered, stunned into not moving.

"Don't get close. You'll want to help me, and I can't be helped." Pacer wet his lips, and Clint saw that some of his brother's teeth were broken off. "I've been killed already. Just stubborn about dying. Wanted to follow you." He coughed slightly, struggling to bring air into his body. "Make sure you were all right."

"Pacer, for God's sake!"

Clint moved forward and his brother backed the horse away from him. "Don't try, Clint. Sometimes . . . sometimes it's seemed to me the only worth-while thing I could do in this life would be to die." He took another long, shuddering breath, then after a time continued. "Will

123

you—will you live for me, Clint? Will you keep some thought or idea or feeling I've had? Keep it in you—and maybe pass it on to your kids?"

"Stop it, Pacer! Please!" Clint stepped forward.

Pacer wheeled the sorrel a few yards away from Clint. There was a faint smile on his lips now. "Last night, Clint—last night when I was fighting off the . . . other Kiowas, I saw the Black Star of Death." He shrugged in answer to a formless question. "I know you don't believe it, but Ma . . ." He shook his head slowly and looked down at the ground. "I got to last long enough to go high into the hills and die. I'll trust you to honor my wish, Clint."

He rode away at a lope, sitting the sorrel by sheer force of will and spirit.

"Pacer!" Clint called loudly after him, limping after him hopelessly. He stopped and shouted more desperately, "Pacer! *Pacer!*"

But there was nothing he could do to stop his brother. Clint stood alone on the prairie, helpless, as Pacer disappeared over the crest of the gently rising slope. And he knew in his helplessness that his younger brother was dying and that he would honor Pacer's last wish.

He didn't know how long he had stood there alone on the wide flat when he heard Roslyn's voice behind him. "What can I do?"

In a low tone he said, "Will you get me a horse?" He did not turn around.

She said, "You're . . . are you the only one left?"

He nodded, his back still to her.

"And you're never coming here again?"

"No."

After a pause she said, "These people may have misjudged, but they did what they thought was right."

"They were wrong." He turned toward her now. "Are you going to get me a horse? I'd like not to set foot in The Crossing again."

"Yes." She turned and walked quickly away.

It was her own horse that she brought back to him, saddled and ready to go. He took the reins from her hand and said, "What's he worth? Him and his furniture?"

"Why?"

"So I can send you the money for him."

She said in a low fury, "Don't you talk to me like that! He's yours!"

Clint pulled himself into the left stirrup and slowly eased his right leg over the horse's rump and into place. "I'm sorry."

"Can't you find it in you to stay?"

"And put up posters saying Clint Burton is clean now? That the Kiowa stain has been washed off him?"

Tears glinted in her eyes. "You're—right now you're worse than we were!"

"I've reason."

"So did we, but they were wrong, stupid reasons. Being stupid has got to stop somewhere!" She turned and ran back across the flat so that he would not see her tears.

It was late night when Clint got to Flaming Lance. He had not known what to expect there and was surprised to find the buildings intact. The only change was that the horses had been run off. He did not know that Buffalo Horn had ordered no damage done to this place and that even in death Buffalo Horn's authority had been recognized by his warriors. Yet taking horses did not actually damage a place.

There was one horse in the corral, the sorrel that Pacer had been on as he rode away. The sorrel had wandered through the open gate and was waiting to be fed. Riding close, Clint saw that the animal was now without bridle. Pacer had taken the bridle off before sending the horse away.

Clint hazed the animal out of the corral, pulling the gate shut on the now empty enclosure. "Go on and be free," he told the sorrel. It did not want to be free so much as it wanted to be fed, and Clint had to swat it to send it loping resentfully out toward the flats.

Riding out toward Buckskin Pass, where Pacer had held down the Kiowas long enough to keep them off his brother's back, Clint counted five stone burial mounds that had been hastily thrown up over dead braves.

At last he rode back, knowing what he had to do.

Three good people gone. Horses stolen. Cattle scattered God knew where over the country. Clint could not, would not, stay in this land where the neighboring people were as they were. The Burtons might have handled marauding warriors alone, but they could not stand off the attack that came from both sides at once.

All because of what people thought! And Clint realized, with grim hatred of the fact, how insidious and dangerous a man's thoughts can be. For though they were invisible and weightless, they put a man into action, whatever that action might be.

Not only could Clint not stay at Flaming Lance, but he could not allow future strangers to desecrate the work of twenty years put in by his mother and father. That was why he knew with finality what he had to do.

The sorrel had wandered back to stand near the corral, and Clint said, "All right. I'll feed you, but I'll put you to work."

He fed both horses a good amount of grain, then went into the house and lighted candles. He gathered a few personal things together, including a tintype of the four Burtons that had been taken seven years before when a wandering photographer had passed through The Crossing. Not having a rifle now, he took the Collier's over-and-under from its pegs, and he took the few hundred dollars in gold, which would be of no use to the others now. He took some food.

When he'd made up a bedroll of these things and lashed the roll to the sorrel, he returned to the house for one last time. He admired the stoutness and comfort of it, and he ran his fingers over the table Sam had built, standing silently for a long moment.

Roused by a small gust of wind that puffed dust into the open doorway, Clint straightened up, then strode across the room to where the kerosene can was stored. He spilled kerosene over the place and then threw a lighted match into the house from the doorway.

126

He fired the hay in the barn, and, riding a short distance away, leading the sorrel, he watched the flames mount higher and higher. He did not know how long he sat there watching, his face set in stony lines.

A movement to his left caused him to whirl, his hand coming up with the Colt in it. It was Roslyn, and she was riding slowly into the circle of light toward him.

"How'd you get here?"

Her voice was small and scared, and her eyes moved from him to the flaming, crackling buildings. "Pa and Angus brought me."

He stared into the darkness beyond her. "If they come into the light, I'll shoot them."

"I guess they know that. They stayed way back."

He put his gun away. "What do you want?"

"To be with you."

Clint nodded into the darkness and said slowly, "Do they know that?"

"Yes." Then her words came in a rush. "Maybe I haven't understood, and done the wrong thing sometimes, but I tried—I tried, and that's something!" Her voice trembled. "We had an understanding, and I went into it honestly and with feeling. And right now, you need someone—need someone more than most men ever do!"

The fire was now rising to its peak over both the house and the barn.

Clint stared away from the high, curling flames and at an angle to the west where the moon dimly outlined the higher peaks of the range of mountains beyond. He wondered which of them Pacer had gone to, to die in lonely pride rather than throw himself on the mercy of the people in The Crossing, and he remembered what Pacer had said—about Clint living for him.

"Roslyn, I don't know where I'm going, and I don't know what I'm going to do." His voice grew husky. "And I am Pacer's brother. Never think of me as his half-brother. Never expect more, or less, of me than you'd have expected of him.

"If you can accept me on those terms, then welcome, and maybe there is hope." He turned his horse abruptly and rode away leading the sorrel.

Roslyn twisted briefly in the saddle to stare out into the dark where she knew her father and Angus were waiting. She could see nothing, so she did not raise her hand in farewell.

She turned her horse and followed after Clint, riding out of the light thrown by the flames and into the cooler, dim-silver light cast by the moon.